SO-AEZ-553

The Mighty Mississippi

While the twins were wrestling, Davy plucked Bartleby out of his bowl and held him up to the TV. "Look, Bart," he whispered. "That river's your real home. It's called the Mighty Mississippi."

Mostly television showed things Bartleby didn't understand. But when he saw the red-eared turtles swimming in the fast-flowing brownish water, he felt a strange pulling sensation inside. His webbed feet began to paddle in Davy's palm.

Red-eared turtles like to dine on duckweed or hunt for insects and small fish.

Bartleby stared harder at the TV. A tiny silver fin was poking out of the mouth of one of the TV turtles. Bartleby felt a mysterious, tangy sensation on his own tongue. His feet paddled faster.

"Hey, Davy, what are you doing?" Jeff poked his head out from under Josh. "That pinhead can't watch TV. His eyes probably aren't even connected to his brain."

"Yes, he can." Davy held out his palm. "Look, he's trying to swim into the picture."

OTHER BOOKS YOU MAY ENJOY

Gentle Ben	Walt Morey
The *Hank the Cowdog* series	John R. Erickson
Kavik the Wolf Dog	Walt Morey
Lad: A Dog	Albert Terhune
The Midnight Fox	Betsy Byars
My Side of the Mountain	Jean Craighead George
The 101 Dalmatians	Dodie Smith
Pigs Might Fly	Dick King-Smith
Rabbit Hill	Robert Lawson
Rascal	Sterling North

BARTLEBY
of the Mighty Mississippi

*To Scotland School –
Students
Read! Read! Read!*

[signature]

BARTLEBY
of the Mighty Mississippi

PHYLLIS SHALANT

with illustrations by **ANNA VOJTECH**

PUFFIN BOOKS

PUFFIN BOOKS
Published by Penguin Group
Penguin Young Readers Group,
345 Hudson Street, New York, New York 10014, U.S.A.
Penguin Books Ltd, 80 Strand, London WC2R ORL, England
Penguin Books Australia Ltd, 250 Camberwell Road,
Camberwell, Victoria 3124, Australia
Penguin Books Canada Ltd, 10 Alcorn Avenue, Toronto, Ontario, Canada M4V 3B2
Penguin Books (N.Z.) Ltd, 182-190 Wairau Road, Auckland 10, New Zealand

First published in the United States of America by Dutton Children's Books,
a division of Penguin Putnam Books for Young Readers, 2000
Published by Puffin Books,
a division of Penguin Young Readers Group, 2004

1 3 5 7 9 10 8 6 4 2

Text copyright © Phyllis Shalant, 2000
Illustrations copyright Anna Vojtech, 2000
All rights reserved

THE LIBRARY OF CONGRESS HAS CATALOGED THE DUTTON EDITION AS FOLLOWS:
Shalant, Phyllis.
Bartleby of the mighty Mississippi/Phyllis Shalant.—1st ed.   p.   cm.
Summary: After being abandoned in a pond, Bartleby, a pet turtle, meets many other
creatures, learns to survive in the wild, and decides to go in search of his birthplace.
ISBN 0-525-46033-0
1. Turtles—Juvenile fiction. [1. Turtles—Fiction. 2. Pond animals—Fiction.
3. Animals—Fiction.]
PZ10.3.S38425 Bar 2000 [Fic]—dc21 99-089893

Puffin Books ISBN 0-14-230025-X

Printed in the United States of America

Except in the United States of America, this book is sold subject to the condition that
it shall not, by way of trade or otherwise, be lent, re-sold, hired out, or otherwise
circulated without the publisher's prior consent in any form of binding or cover
other than that in which it is published and without a similar condition
including this condition being imposed on the subsequent purchaser.

For Donna Brooks

CONTENTS

1	SPINACH DAY	3
2	CHUTES AND LADDERS	6
3	*NATURAL WORLD*	11
4	FOOD OR FOE?	16
5	DEAD MAN'S FLOAT	19
6	HOMESICK	27
7	A-HUNTING WE WILL GO	34
8	THE WAYS OF A TURTLE	39
9	CRUNCHY, CHEWY, JUICY, GOOEY	43
10	OTHERS!	50
11	SLIP!	56
12	SSSEEZER	60
13	THE CLAW, THE PAW, AND THE JAW	65
14	FRIEND	71
15	SURPRISES UNDER THE WATER	76
16	LITTLE GREEN EGGLET	83
17	FIVE	91
18	JUNKET	96
19	SSSLIP!	102

20 EGGLET-SITTING   106

21 OLD FRIEND   109

22 THE TRADE   114

23 DARK JOURNEY   117

24 TRAPPED!   123

25 THE INVITATION   127

26 BROTHER-*WAK*!   133

27 THROUGH THE WOODS   139

28 PAST THE HUMANS' HOUSES   145

29 ACROSS THE SCHOOL YARD   148

30 THE FIELD OF HOLES   152

31 THE GREAT ROAD   156

32 TAIL'S END   160

PART One

Spinach Day

1

Bartleby was basking peacefully in the light of the ginger-jar lamp when the hand grabbed him from his bowl. It had long, fishy-white fingers. The fingers had sharp red nails. Bartleby pulled his head and limbs into his shell. He knew who the hand belonged to. He knew what was coming next.

"Okay, little turtle, time for your bath," the mother said. "We don't want the boys getting salmonella disease from you, do we?" The hand carried Bartleby into the bathroom and set him down in the sink. Cold water began trickling from the faucet above him. Next came a slick, sweet-smelling substance.

"First we'll do your carapace."

A stiff brush scrubbed the top of Bartleby's shell. Inside, he shut his eyes and mouth. The worst part was coming—the upside-down part. It always made Bartleby dizzy.

Sure enough, the fingers turned him over. "Now your

plastron." The brush scoured the underside of his shell. Bartleby felt as if he could hardly breathe.

Finally, the trickling water became a forceful shower. It pelted his shell and oozed inside while the hand turned him this way and that.

"There. Now you're nice and fresh. Just stay here in the sink while I get you some lettuce."

Bartleby hated the too-sweet odor that clung to his shell, but at the mention of lettuce his spirits perked up. He hoped the mother would bring him the delicious, dark green leaves instead of the pale, crunchy kind.

"Spinach—you're in luck today." The white fingers poked a broad, flat leaf in his face. "Come on out and eat. Nummy, nummy! I'm going to change the water in your bowl. Stay right there!"

As if I could go anywhere else, Bartleby thought. He waited until she was gone to ease his head out. Then he gulped the air to test the smell of the leaf. Its fresh, sharp scent reminded Bartleby of the breezes that drifted in when the mother opened the window near his bowl. He nudged the leaf with his head. It was smooth and springy. He opened his mouth and took a bite. The taste was deliciously bitter on his tongue. This was wonderful lettuce!

"Time to go back to your bowl now, little Red-ear." The fingers plucked Bartleby out of the sink.

"Wait! I'm not finished. I want more!" Bartleby tried to signal the mother by scrabbling his feet against her palm.

"Why, aren't you cute? Are you excited because the boys will be home in a few minutes?" the mother asked.

Bartleby quickly pulled in his neck, head, feet, and tail. He willed himself to become a stone. That was his only answer.

Chutes and Ladders

2

"Let's play Monopoly!" Jeff shouted, running into the living room.

"Okay, I'll be the race car," answered his twin brother, Josh.

"I want to play, too! I'll be the shoe!" Davy, their little brother, bounced up and down like a yo-yo.

In his bowl on the end table, Bartleby felt the boys' vibrations. Slowly, he emerged from his turtle nap. He hated giving up his dream. He'd been floating in a big water place. There'd been warm sunlight on his back and cool water under his webs. He'd been rocking gently from side to side. He'd felt wonderful. Then the boys had arrived.

Bartleby peered at Jeff. The boy pushed back the thin patch of brown fur on his head and sighed loudly. He looked down at Davy through the little eye windows that were balanced on his nose.

"You can't play Monopoly, Davy. You have to be able

to read and count money. You're only five. Why don't you go watch cartoons."

Bartleby knew what came next. He felt like pulling his head in. But then he would miss seeing Davy's amazing trick.

Sure enough, big drops of rain began to fall from the little boy's eyes. "I want to! I want to! It's not fair!" Davy screamed. "You have to let me play!"

"Davy, stop! Let go of my leg! Mom, would you get him off me!"

"Boys, come have a snack, I've got brownies," the mother called. To Bartleby's relief, Davy and the twins ran out of the living room.

Bartleby settled down and tried to return to his turtle nap. He basked in the heat of the ginger-jar lamp and waited for the floaty feeling to come.

Sometimes during a turtle nap, Bartleby saw things he didn't understand. He heard buzzing, hissing, or bubbling. He gulped scents—sweet or smelly. He felt himself drifting, weightless as a fly's wing. He was just settling into a new nap when a sticky hand plucked him up.

"I'm playing Chutes and Ladders with Bart!" Davy shouted.

"Mom, tell him to put Bartleby back!" Jeff called.

Yes, Mom, maybe you'd better, Bartleby silently agreed. He hadn't forgotten the last time Davy had taken him outside. Bartleby had loved treading on the fresh, bouncy grass. He'd loved the feel of sunshine on his shell.

7

But then Davy had shoved him into the pocket of his jacket and forgotten about him until the next morning. The long, dark time in the scratchy cloth pocket had been terrifying.

"Oh, honey, let Davy play with Bartleby," the mother called back. "He loves that turtle. He won't hurt him."

Bartleby felt himself squeezed inside Davy's fist and carried along. When the fist uncurled, Bartleby recognized Davy's place. It was smaller than the place where his bowl was kept, and it was stuffed with playthings. He hoped Davy wasn't going to give him a ride in the dune buggy thing again. Last time, Davy had pushed the dune buggy so hard that it had crashed into the wall. For a long while afterward, Bartleby had felt dizzy and sick.

Playing with Davy's stiff little humans was even worse. Sometimes the boy lined them up and made Bartleby be something called a tank. Then he pushed Bartleby into them until they'd all been knocked over.

"Here, boy, try this brownie." Davy set Bartleby down on the plate he had been carrying.

Bartleby liked the brownie's dirtlike color. He sniffed and gulped to smell it. The scent was strange and mysterious. He nudged it with his head. The brownie felt squishy. Bartleby took a small bite.

Yuck! The brownie left a fuzzy coating on his tongue. Disgusting! It was so sweet, it made his throat hurt. How could Davy like the stuff?

Bartleby looked over at Davy's bed and shuddered.

There was Spike, the green, silent creature with the long, flat snout and rows of spiky teeth. Bartleby knew it was a plaything—it never moved or even blinked. Still, there was something about Spike that meant danger.

"I'll be this boy with the brown hair, and you can be the one with the yellow hair, Bart," Davy was saying now. He was on his knees on the floor, unfolding a game board. "Hey, where's the spinner? I lost the spinner!" He looked under his bed. He poked through the wastebasket. Then he shrugged. "Oh well, Bart. I guess you'll have to be the spinner."

The next thing Bartleby knew, he was lying on his back in the middle of the game board. He began paddling the air with his feet.

Davy flicked a finger and sent Bartleby spinning. "Whee! Point, Bart! Point to a number."

Bartleby felt confused and panicky. He pulled his head, limbs, and tail into his shell. Something sharp followed him inside and pricked his tail.

"Tickle, tickle with my pencil," Davy said. "Point to six, Bart."

Bartleby tucked in more tightly. The sharp thing touched his head.

"Come on, Bart! Point!"

"Hey, what are you doing?" Bartleby heard Davy's brother Jeff.

"I'm trying to teach Bart to point to a number."

"You can't teach him numbers, Davy. You can't teach

him anything." Bartleby felt himself being snatched up roughly. "Don't you know? He's dumb as a stone. He's just a stupid little turtle!"

Back in his bowl, Bartleby didn't come out of his shell for the rest of the afternoon. He didn't try to search for leftover flakes in his water or return to his turtle nap. He lay on the bottom exactly where he'd been dropped. Like a dumb little stone.

Natural World 3

Jeff was the first one in the living room after dinner. He grabbed the remote control and spread himself over exactly half of the maroon-flowered couch. "Hey, Josh, hurry! *Natural World's* coming on. Maybe they'll have the show on dinosaurs again."

"Yeah, or the one on ant wars!" Josh raced into the living room carrying a bag of chips and plopped down on the other half of the couch. The title of tonight's show was already coming on the screen: TURTLES OF THE MIGHTY MISSISSIPPI.

"Hey! Maybe that's where Bartleby comes from," Josh said.

"Yeah, the Mighty Mississippi—or a puddle." Both boys snickered.

Bartley wasn't listening. He was turtle napping. Instead of the dull puddle in his bowl, he was paddling in a big water place. It was so deep, his webs couldn't feel the bottom!

11

"Over two hundred million years ago, the first true turtles appeared," the narrator said.

"Wow! Did you hear that?" Jeff pushed his glasses up on his nose. "That means Bartleby's relatives were around even before dinosaurs!"

"Yeah, turtles are old, all right. Maybe that's why they smell so bad." Josh glanced over at the turtle bowl and held his nose.

But Bartleby didn't see. He was still paddling in the big water place. Suddenly, he felt a stirring behind him. Something nipped at his rear web! He pulled away.

On the screen, a scientist displayed a fossil of an enormous turtle. *Prehistoric* Archelon *was ten feet long and weighed two tons,* she said.

"Hey!" Josh pointed to the TV. "That turtle looks like the substitute teacher we had last week, Mrs. Potluck!"

"Ha! Her dandruff flakes were bigger than Bartleby's turtle-food flakes," Jeff said. He thumped the couch. "Hey, maybe that's what turtle food is made from—dandruff!"

"Bart, look, a big turtle! Maybe it's your grandpa," Davy called from the doorway.

Inside his dream, Bartleby heard Davy calling him. He tried to ignore the boy. He wanted to stay in the big water place.

"Bart, don't you want to see your friends? Look!"

It was no use. Bartleby began to awaken. The flickering shadows of the big water place flowed into the flickering light of the TV screen.

A giant turtle came swimming forward. It had a huge hooked jaw and jagged points sticking up from its shell.

"Maybe we can feed Davy to one of those!" Jeff slapped his knee.

"I'll feed *you* to that turtle," Davy said to Jeff. He stomped across the carpet. "Move over, I want to sit."

"No room."

Davy crossed his arms and stood right in front of the couch, blocking the twins' view.

"Move over, I can't see!" Jeff shoved Davy with his foot.

While the boys fought, Bartleby gazed at the TV. He flicked his stubby tail back and forth. He blinked. There was another turtle!

Sternotherus oderatus is more commonly known as the stinkpot turtle. It exudes vile-smelling secretions when disturbed.

"Look, Davy, it's you! A stinkpot!" Jeff shouted.

Josh laughed so hard, he fell off the couch.

A splashing sound made Bartleby press his snout against his bowl so he could see better. Inside the TV was a row of bright-eyed turtles. Each one had a bar of red on either side of its head. One by one, they were slipping off a log into a big water place.

When diving, the red-eared turtle functions like a miniature submarine.

Bartleby scrabbled up the side of his bowl, balancing on his hind legs.

"Hey!" Davy shouted. "Those turtles look just like Bart!"

"See, I was right. Bartleby *is* from the Mighty Mississippi," Josh said. He picked up a couch pillow and bopped Jeff on the head.

Jeff conked him back. "Yeah. Bartleby of the Mighty Mississippi," he snorted.

While the twins were wrestling, Davy plucked Bartleby out of his bowl and held him up to the TV. "Look, Bart," he whispered. "That river's your real home. It's called the Mighty Mississippi."

Mostly television showed things Bartleby didn't understand. But when he saw the red-eared turtles swimming in the fast-flowing brownish water, he felt a strange pulling sensation inside. His webbed feet began to paddle in Davy's palm.

Red-eared turtles like to dine on duckweed or hunt for insects and small fish.

Bartleby stared harder at the TV. A tiny silver fin was poking out of the mouth of one of the TV turtles. Bartleby felt a mysterious, tangy sensation on his own tongue. His feet paddled faster.

"Hey, Davy, what are you doing?" Jeff poked his head out from under Josh. "That pinhead can't watch TV. His eyes probably aren't even connected to his brain."

"Yes, he can." Davy held out his palm. "Look, he's trying to swim into the picture."

"Ha-ha," Josh snickered. "That's the funniest thing I ever heard."

"Bart can dive and hunt. The guy said he's like a submarine," Davy insisted.

"Right, Bartleby the Submarine." Josh snatched Bartleby from Davy's open palm and ran around the room. "Look, Bartleby the Submarine can fly, too."

Bartleby wanted to see more of the turtles. But the motion of flying through the air was making him dizzy. Miserably, he tucked in his head and limbs. When Josh finally stopped, he peeked out again, but there was only a human in the TV now.

Good-bye for now from our Natural World *to yours!* the human said.

"Here's your natural world, pinhead," Josh sneered. He dropped Bartleby into the inch-deep water in his bowl and shook out some flakes of turtle food. A few landed on Bartleby's shell and stuck there.

"Have some dandruff, pinhead."

Food or Foe? 4

The lights were out, but Bartleby couldn't sleep. He was still thinking about the fast, brown water called the Mighty Mississippi and the red-eared turtles who lived there.

He wished he could ask them what it felt like to swim in such fast water. He stretched out his rear webs, pretending he was pushing against the flow. Whitish moonlight came through the window and lit up Bartleby's own water place. A tiny, shallow puddle. He closed his eyes so he wouldn't have to look at it.

After a while he felt the floaty feeling. He saw brownish water flowing over and under him. He felt a lightness and a swiftness that made his heart beat faster.

Colors and images came to him. Some he recognized as plants. They seemed to be reaching for him. Others were creatures that could swim and dart and fly. Their voices were a myriad of chirrupings, croakings, peepings, and bellowings.

16

He saw a great dark tunnel—a strange tunnel. It looked like two long, sharp teeth were hanging from its roof. Bartleby shuddered. He tried to resist the tunnel, but he couldn't slow down. . . .

The next morning, a cheerful chirping woke him. Bartleby felt much better. A light breeze tickled his carapace and rippled the water in his bowl. The mother didn't usually keep the window open, but today it was pushed way up. Bartleby gulped. So many new smells! Damp, green, mouthwatering odors. He wanted to fill himself up with them.

He gazed toward the open window. The sun streamed in at a new angle. Bartleby sensed the world outdoors was changing. He felt changed himself. He slipped into his water and waded from one side of his bowl to the other.

The front door slammed, and Davy came running into the room. "Bart, look! I found you something to eat! Go on—bite its head off!"

Bartleby stared at the long, squirmy strand dangling in front of him. It was smooth and twitchy. Suddenly the strand jerked itself free of Davy's fingers. It fell into the water and began writhing horribly. Bartleby ducked into his shell.

"Aw, Bart, you're not afraid of a dumb earthworm, are you? Come on! Eat it!"

Bartleby watched the horrible strand wriggle and twist. He didn't move.

"Oh, Bart!" Davy picked up the strand and swung it away. "Don't you know you're supposed to eat worms? You're not even a real turtle!"

Inside his shell Bartleby felt something shrinking. The feeling was worse than being dropped, or squeezed, or even flipped onto his carapace and spun around.

Not a real turtle—that's what Davy had said.

If I'm not a real turtle, what am I? Bartleby wondered. He shut his eyes, but he didn't feel like dreaming.

Dead Man's Float

5

Later, Bartleby watched the sun sink slowly behind the trees. He listened to the birds sing their final songs of the day. It was almost time for the boys to swoop into the living room and settle in front of the TV. Instead, he heard them scrambling in the coat closet. Then the front door slammed.

Soon Jeff's voice came drifting through the open window. "I'll bat first!"

"Okay. How about I pitch you ten and then we switch?" That was Josh.

"What about me? When is it my turn?"

"You don't get one, Davy. Our first game's this weekend. We've got to practice."

"That's not fair!"

"You can play outfield, Davy."

"No! I want a turn to bat!"

"Give me the ball, Davy!"

"No!"

"Davy . . ."

"Ow! Stop grabbing! Hey!"

Bartleby guessed from Davy's squeals that his eyes were making rain again. In a moment, the front door slammed once more. Davy stomped into the living room and stood in front of Bartleby's bowl, sniffling. He put a grubby finger into the water and stirred.

"They never let me play with them, Bart."

Bartleby stretched his neck out to show he was listening.

"They think both of us are too little to do anything. But we're not, right, boy?"

Bartleby scrabbled down the ramp into his cloudy puddle. He wanted Davy to turn on the TV.

Davy watched Bartleby plop into the shallow water. "That's right, boy. You can swim better than Jeff and Josh. You can even swim across a giant river." Suddenly, Davy lifted Bartleby up. "Hey, want to try it?"

Bartleby couldn't stop his webs from paddling in Davy's palm. Was the boy really going to take him to the big water place? Bartleby squinched himself into his shell as Davy stuffed him inside a jacket pocket.

The door slammed again. Through the fabric of Davy's jacket, the air felt cooler. Bartleby quivered with excitement. They were outside!

"Hey, Davy, where are you going?"

"To see if Amy wants to play baseball with me."

"Mom's letting you go around the corner by yourself?"

"Yes!"

"But it'll be dark soon."

Bartleby was confused. He liked Davy's friend Amy. Once, she'd fed him a bite of a tiny, tasty tree she called broccoli. But weren't they going to the Mighty Mississippi? Wasn't that what Davy had said?

Bartleby jiggled in Davy's pocket as the boy began walking faster.

"Hey, Davy! If you're going to play ball, where's your mitt?"

"I'll use Amy's." Bartleby began to bounce up and down as Davy broke into a run.

"Almost there, boy." Through the jacket, Bartleby could feel Davy's fingers patting him. The bobbing and jostling was making him dizzy. Finally, it stopped.

"Okay, boy," Davy whispered. "We made it. The trail's up ahead."

From inside Davy's pocket, Bartleby concentrated on every sound. Davy's panting. Snapping and rustling. Buzzing, chirping, and chattering.

"Here we are, boy." Davy came to a stop and pulled Bartleby out of his pocket. "Look!" He lifted Bartleby up to see.

Bartleby blinked in amazement. The big water place before him was shiny and dark. It was surrounded by plants of every size and shade of green. And yet, it was very still—not at all like the furiously rushing water Bartleby had seen on TV.

Perhaps the water is napping now, he told himself. Perhaps it will wake up later.

Davy crouched down in the mud. "Okay, Bart, first I'll let you feel it." Without letting go, he dipped Bartleby into the cool water. Bartleby's webbed feet began to push.

"Want to try the dead man's float now? It's easy."

Davy let go, and Bartleby felt the chilly water rocking beneath him. It lapped over his shell as if it would swallow him up. His webs began to push harder. To his amazement, the big water held him up!

"Wow, Bart! You're not just a beginner. You're an advanced beginner!" Davy exclaimed.

Bartleby kept paddling. He moved forward a little, but mostly he just bobbed up and down. The big water made him feel light and free. If this was the dead man's float, he liked it!

"Come on, Bart, swim around!" With an open palm, Davy patted the water next to Bartleby.

Bartleby paddled faster as the small waves rocked him. He moved his tail back and forth, trying to balance.

"That's right, Bart, swim! Swim across the Mighty Mississippi!" Davy stretched his arms out wide and waded deeper into the water.

Bigger waves rocked Bartleby. He wished the boy would pick him up now. His legs were beginning to tire. But when Davy leaned over, he only grabbed a twig that was floating nearby.

"Da-veee! Da-veee! Where are you?"

"Uh-oh. That's Mom, Bart."

"Da-vee! Answer me, please!"

"Hey, Davy! If you're in there, you'd better come out now!"

"Yeah, or else me 'n' Josh will come in and get you!"

Davy dragged the twig through the water, making big S curves. "They didn't let me play ball. I don't have to let them swim with us. Right, boy?"

Bartleby spun helplessly as Davy swirled the twig. He wished the boy would answer the mother's call. He was getting awfully chilly. He needed to go home and have a turtle nap.

"Da-veee! Where are you? Come on home, honey!"

Davy was practically waist-deep now. He looked back over his shoulder. "It's getting late, Bart," he murmured. "We're not supposed to be out after dark, you know."

"Da-vee! Are you lost? Don't be afraid!"

Davy splashed the water with a fist. "We're not babies! We're not afraid! Right, Bart?"

Bartleby stretched his neck out. The sun was slipping lower, leaving pinkish-purple streaks behind it. Here at the Mighty Mississippi, the sky seemed more beautiful. More big and scary, too.

"Da-vee, are you in there? Please answer! You're scaring me!"

Davy looked down at his wet clothes. "That's Mom, Bart. She's going to be awfully mad when she finds me. Maybe we'd better hide."

"Da-vee, please, please answer!"

Davy sighed. "I guess we better tell her we're okay." He leaned over and scooped Bartleby up. Then he began dragging himself out of the pond, his wet clothes trailing little streams of water.

"Davy, come on out already!"

"Yeah, Davy! If you don't, we're gonna take all your stuff. Your dune buggy, your action figures, your stuffed alligator, and—"

"Shut up, will ya, Jeff!"

Just at the water's edge, Davy stopped. "You're lucky, Bart. You don't have any dumb brothers. Or a mom who thinks you're a baby. You can do whatever you want." Suddenly he turned back around. "Hey, Bart, you want to take a last swim? I'll go get Josh and Jeff. Wait till they see what a good swimmer you are. Better than them!" Davy drew back his arm and tossed Bartleby out as far as he could. Then he disappeared down the trail.

PART **TWO**

Homesick

6

Bartleby felt himself floating. He opened his eyes and stuck out his head. The big water was all around him. But it was dark now—and chilly. His limbs felt so stiff, he couldn't help wishing for his ginger-jar lamp. And for home.

Suddenly he remembered how Davy had tossed him into the water like a plaything the boy was tired of. Bartleby felt an ache inside his plastron. He listened for Davy's call. But although he heard peeps and hoots, squeaks and croaks, and a jumble of other sounds, he didn't hear Davy. He reminded himself that Davy had forgotten him before. At least this time he'd been left in a place where he could breathe easily.

"In the morning, Davy will remember me," Bartleby told himself. "Then he'll be back. I'll just swim to shore and wait for him in the clearing place between the trees."

But where was the clearing place? Bartleby tried to look around, but when he paddled his webs, he only moved forward. He tried stretching his neck to one side so his body would follow. But he still moved forward. Finally, he used his tail. He found that if he pointed it in one direction as he paddled, his body would turn the other way.

All he could see onshore were the dim shapes of trees and bushes. In the dark they looked like giant, lumpy creatures. Bartleby shuddered. He was cold and tired and frightened. And he was dizzy from paddling in circles. I'll just swim somewhere and wait, he decided. When the sun comes again, Davy will surely find me.

In the morning, bright light woke Bartleby and made him squint inside his shell. Instead of doors slamming and boys fighting, he heard chirping and rustling. He poked his head out. He was enclosed in a tangle of tall grass. With a forefoot he pushed it away and saw the biggest water place he'd ever seen. Water that was dark, shimmery, and greenish gray. Water that was rippling, swaying, and wonderful. Water that was the Mighty Mississippi!

But where was Davy? At home, the boys would be fighting over cereal boxes. They would be tearing through the house looking for books and shoes. They would be banging out the door.

"I never dreamed the Mighty Mississippi would be so beautiful—or so lonely," Bartleby said to himself. "I thought there would be other creatures."

"What do you think I am?" a grumbly voice asked.

Bartleby looked around. He didn't see anyone. He opened his mouth and gulped anxiously. Something smelled like rotting leaves and human garbage. Quickly, Bartleby snapped his mouth shut.

"Are you deaf?" the voice muttered. "Or just rude?"

"I . . . I thought I might be dreaming," Bartleby replied. "Where are you?"

"Just a moment." Under the shallow water in front of Bartleby's tuft of grass, the mud began to stir. It wriggled and rocked and rose up in a roundish lump. Four webbed feet poked out from under the lump. Then the feet plodded deeper into the water and the whole muddy clod disappeared.

As Bartleby watched in amazement, a turtle bobbed up in its place. It had a smooth carapace and a short, pointy tail. Along either side of its head was a sleek white stripe. Bartleby thought the turtle quite handsome.

"I am *Sternotherus oderatus,*" the turtle announced.

Bartleby gasped—and smelled the bad odor again. "You're a stinkpot!"

"That is only a common appellation. I prefer my Latin name. But you may call me Mudly. I come from a fine family of mud and musk turtles."

Bartleby drew his head in a bit. "I am Bartleby. I come from a family of boys."

"Really?" Mudly paddled closer to the marsh grass. He floated in front of Bartleby and examined his head, the size of his shell, and the thickness of his tail. "You look like a turtle to me."

"I am a turtle—from the Mighty Mississippi. Just like you."

"What do you mean?" A faint trace of foul air wafted from under Mudly's shell.

"I mean that we are both from the Mississippi River," Bartleby replied. "The big water place where we are right now."

Mudly snapped his jaws. "The Mississippi River? Ha! This place is only a pond. A river's long and snaky. It's fast like a flood." He squinted down his snout at Bartleby. "Don't you know anything?"

Bartleby pulled his head halfway into his shell. "I know my real home is the Mighty Mississippi. I heard it on TV."

"What's TV?" Mudly asked.

Bartleby stuck his head out again. So this smelly turtle didn't know everything after all. "A TV is a box with an eye so big it can see anywhere. It can talk, too."

"You don't say." Mudly floated quietly for a moment. His head was up as if he were listening for something. "I'm hungry. How about eating?"

Bartleby was hungry, too. He hadn't eaten a single flake last night. He felt a sudden pang at the thought of home and his bowl. "Do you have any lettuce?" he asked.

"What's lettuce?"

"Flat green leaves. Wide and tender." Bartleby's jaws quivered at the thought.

"We have plenty of wide green leaves around here," Mudly said. "Big, little, smooth, hairy, round, oval, curly—which kind did you mean?"

Bartleby was so overwhelmed, he couldn't reply.

"Actually, in the morning I prefer to hunt," Mudly said. "There's nothing like a live meal to give a turtle energy."

Bartleby looked at the stinkpot more carefully. Mudly was bigger than the mother's hand. Bartleby himself was so small he could fit easily inside Davy's hand. "A live meal?" he asked. "I don't think I've ever had one."

Mudly snapped the air in amazement. "No flies? No gnats or mosquitoes or fleas? No larvae or aphids or worms? But what do you hunt?"

Bartleby felt like disappearing into the marsh grass. Instead, he answered truthfully, "All I've ever eaten are dried flakes and lettuce leaves." He dropped his voice to a whisper. "I've been a pet."

"But you said you were from a river. The Mighty Mississippi."

"I am. At least, I believe that is my true home."

Mudly fished up a bit of leaf that was drifting by and chewed it slowly. "You need to learn how to hunt and forage. Come with me and I'll show you how."

Bartleby hesitated. If he went with Mudly, how would Davy find him?

"What's wrong? Is my scent offending you?" Mudly asked. "It happens whenever I meet someone new. Or when I'm nervous. I'm afraid I can't help it."

"It's not that," Bartleby replied. "I was going to wait here for Davy—my boy." At the thought of Davy, Bartleby felt a sore spot, as if a hard pebble were digging under his plastron.

"You have a boy?" Mudly asked. "You must be very brave."

Bartleby gazed anxiously over the big water. He remembered how chilly it had felt at night, how hard it had been to swim, and how frightened he'd been. He didn't feel very brave at all. "I had three boys where I used to live," he said.

"Three!" Mudly snapped the air in amazement. "The boys I've seen are very dangerous. One of them killed my poor Minerva."

"Who's Minerva?"

"She was going to be the mother of my hatchlings. But one day two boys came here and threw rocks in the water. Big, sharp ones. One of them hit the place in the shallow water where Minerva was hiding. It cracked her shell."

Mudly's sharp scent made Bartleby clamp his mouth shut. "That's awful. But the boys I lived with meant no harm."

"Maybe, maybe not. If I were you, I'd keep away from boys." Mudly paddled around and began swimming out into the deeper water. "Come on, let's go."

Bartleby was starving. "All right. I guess I can look for Davy later on," he said. He pushed the grass out of his way.

"One more thing," Mudly called. "If I were you, I wouldn't tell anyone that you're from the Mighty Mississippi."

"Why not?" Bartleby asked.

But Mudly was already far ahead and didn't seem to hear.

A-Hunting We Will Go

At first, Bartleby paddled after Mudly as hard as he could. But he felt clumsy and awkward, and he couldn't keep up anyway. Soon, he gave up trying. His webs relaxed into a steady rhythm—and his swimming became smoother and easier. It was wonderful!

Still, before long, he was tired. He was afraid he'd be lost in the big water, and he didn't want to be alone again. Finally, Mudly stopped at a place where white flowers floated beside dark green leaves. The leaves looked a lot like lettuce. Bartleby's jaw began to quiver excitedly. He opened his mouth and took a bite.

"Blech!" he exclaimed.

"Serfs you right for trying to eat other creatures' food." A furry, pointy-faced animal swam right by Bartleby. It was carrying one of the leaves in its mouth. Quickly, Bartleby pulled into his shell.

"Don't mind him. That's just Muskrat," Mudly said. "He thinks this entire patch of lily pads is his."

"Izz, too," Muskrat mumbled, his mouth still clamped tightly around the leaf. Bartleby was amazed at how well the furry creature could swim. It looked a bit like the squirrels he used to watch in the tree outside his window—except for its strange, hairless tail.

"That greedy creature tried to chew this leaf right out from under me!" a deep voice complained.

Mudly emitted a foul scent. "At least Muskrat doesn't eat everything in sight like you bigfrogs do, Bully."

Bigfrogs? Bartleby paddled around to see who was speaking. All he detected was the slick, flat water and the bobbing leaves and flowers. Suddenly one of the leaves began kicking its back webs. Bartleby stared in amazement. The leaf was a creature! A creature with a wide, flat head. And big round eyes that looked as if they were about to pop. And a mouth so wide, it stretched from one side of its head to the other.

The mouth opened. "You're just jealous, Stinkpot," the deep voice said. "You'd eat a lot more, too, if you could catch it. When your prey smells you coming, it flees. Why, you even make me want to jump out of this pond!" As if to prove it, the creature leapt out of the water and landed on a lily pad right next to Bartleby.

"What are those red things on the side of your head?" the bigfrog demanded.

"Ear bands," Bartleby said as he back-paddled away. "I'm a red-eared turtle."

"I've never seen one of you around here before. Where's the rest of your family?"

"His kind are loners, too, like us *Sternotherus oderatuses,*" Mudly replied before Bartleby could answer.

"Like you *stinkpots,* you mean."

"I don't think Mudly smells so bad," Bartleby said. He wished the great green bigfrog would leave them alone.

"At least Mudly doesn't keep everyone awake all night with his silly boasting like you bigfrogs do," a dry, rattling voice called from above.

Bartleby stretched his neck up and cocked his head. Sitting on a tree branch over the water was a bird with blazing blue feathers. "You're beautiful!" he exclaimed.

"I'm talented, too," the bird told him. "Would you like to see me catch a fish?"

"Okay," Bartleby replied.

The bird flashed its fancy blue-and-white wings. Then it dove headfirst into the water. In another moment, it came up with a squirming fish in its beak and flew back to the branch.

"Very nice," Bartleby said.

"Oh, Kingfisher's not finished yet," Mudly told him. "Watch."

Bartleby squinted up again at the lovely bird. Suddenly, it jerked its head, whacking the fish against the branch over and over. Triumphantly, the bird tossed its head back and let the fish slip down its white throat.

Bartleby hoped he wouldn't have to beat his prey like

that. Even so, watching the kingfisher eat had made him hungrier than ever. "Mudly, what are we going to hunt?" he asked.

"Little worm very yummy," a soft voice said.

Bartleby peered beneath a water flower and saw a blackish-green creature with yellow spots drifting quietly. He thought it looked like a worm itself, except that it had four legs.

"I don't like worms at all," Bartleby told the shy creature.

"Rrroak?" the bigfrog croaked. "I've never met a turtle who didn't like worms. Where did you say you're from?"

"I didn't say." Bartleby paddled backward, half hiding under a lily pad.

"Well, what do you eat?"

"F . . . flakes," Bartleby said. "Lettuce."

"Never heard of them." The bigfrog hopped to the edge of the floating leaf and eyed Bartleby more closely. "I don't think you're from around here at all."

"I am—sort of. I lived in a house with people just beyond the woods," Bartleby admitted.

"Ha! A pet! I knew it!" the bigfrog bellowed. "We had a pet frog around here once. It was more fearful than that spotted salamander over there. It was even afraid of a worm!"

Bartleby wondered what had happened to that pet. But he didn't ask.

"Oh, go eat a maggot, Bully!" Mudly snapped. "Someday this red-eared turtle will be a fine hunter."

"Ha! That poky little thing? What makes you think so, Stinkpot?"

Bartleby had had enough of this bigfrog's insults. "Because my true home is a great, fast river—a place where the most powerful creatures live. The Mighty Mississippi," he announced, forgetting Mudly's warning.

Suddenly, the beautiful kingfisher flew away. The bigfrog dove off the lily pad. The muskrat swam to shore. The spotted creature vanished without a ripple.

Bartleby paddled around in a circle. "What happened? Where did they all go?" he asked.

Mudly snapped up something from the water's surface and chewed it calmly. "You shouldn't have mentioned the Mighty Mississippi. The name makes them fearful."

"But why?"

"Because of the rumor. If you ask me, there are enough things to worry about without—"

"Rumor? What's that?"

"Hearsay. Unreliable information of uncertain origin. Probably just a tale made up by a skittish creature like the spotted salamander. Not indisputable like hunger—*which I can feel right now!*" Mudly began paddling away. "Come, let us eat!"

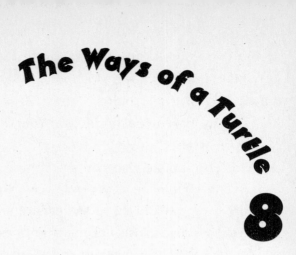

The Ways of a Turtle

8

"Keep low and look carefully," Mudly hissed as he began swimming among the lily pads.

Bartleby struggled to keep his shell beneath the water. Like Mudly, only his eyes and snout showed above the surface. "Look where? At what?" he called.

"Shhh! You'll scare it off." Mudly stopped paddling beside a sweet-smelling blossom. He turned his head toward the flower and held very still.

"Scare who?" Bartleby asked more quietly.

"Food," Mudly whispered. "There, just above the flower."

Bartleby stretched his neck. He blinked and squinted. But he didn't see anything to eat. Mudly's jaws quickly opened and shut. Then he began chewing.

The food here must be invisible, Bartleby thought. His empty stomach filled with despair. "I don't think I know how to look," he said.

"Come along and watch." Mudly began paddling

again. "Do you see that ray of light there beyond the leaves?" He nodded toward a spot of glittering water on the far side of the lily patch.

Bartleby narrowed his eyes. "You mean where it's bright and shiny?"

"Yes. The shimmering you see is more than just sunlight. It's the fluttering of wings. Gnats' wings. Too many to count. You must learn to see each one."

Bartleby stared closely at the brightness. It seemed to pulse and throb. He tried to focus—to follow a single point. But it was like trying to pick out one drop of water in a rain cloud.

"I can't."

"Yes, you can. You have to keep trying," Mudly replied. With his sharp foreclaws he pulled himself onto one of the lily pads. "Persistence is part of being a turtle."

Bartleby tried to copy Mudly. He drifted over to a lily pad and grabbed on with his tiny, sharp foreclaws. But the pad was slippery and jiggly. As soon as he scrambled halfway up—*splash*—he slid back into the water.

Sliding was fun! Bartleby wanted to do it again, but he could smell Mudly releasing his rotten scent. More carefully this time, he tried scaling the leaf. It bobbed up and down a bit, but he clung fast.

He turned his head toward the light stream and squinted until his vision became filled with pure, bright light. He waited. After a while, tiny shapes began to emerge within the beam. Inside, Bartleby felt a fluttery feeling. He saw a tiny, flashing light. Quick as the slightest breath, it disappeared. Bartleby kept perfectly still. He saw another flash, clearer this time—a single pair of wings.

"Mudly, I see one!" he whispered. "Come on! Let's go get it."

"Not so fast," Mudly said. "Listen and tell me what you hear."

Bartleby focused on sounds. "Birds," he answered quickly. "The breeze in the grass. The leaves rustling. The water rippling. And . . . and . . . tiny wings beating everywhere."

Mudly snapped his jaws at the air. "That's right! Mosquitoes, gnats, fleas, moths, mayflies . . . you're hearing your food."

"Is there anything else?" Bartleby asked. He was beginning to feel weak with hunger.

"Touch." Mudly thumped his tall against the lily pad. "You must read the lapping of the water. The whiskings that cross your shell. The movement of mud under your webs." Mudly suddenly stiffened. "Shhh!"

"What is it?" Bartleby asked, alarmed.

"The sweet whine of a mosquito. I'm off for breakfast now—it's getting late. Pleasant eating!" Mudly slipped into the water and began paddling away.

"Wait! Where will I find you?" Bartleby asked.

"You won't—for a while. After eating, I nap under the mud. Alone."

"Oh." Bartleby tried not to sound disappointed.

"In the afternoon I'll be on the basking rock in the middle of the water. If you like, you could join me there," Mudly offered.

The middle of the big water. Bartleby wondered if he would ever be able to swim that far. Or be a real turtle like Mudly. What if he stayed a dumb, helpless pet forever?

"Bartleby! I forgot the most important thing!" Mudly was calling him. "The more you eat, the bigger you get. The bigger you get, the harder you are to swallow!"

Bartleby dug his nails into the lily pad. *"Swallow? Did you say swallow?"* But Mudly had already disappeared.

Crunchy, Chewy, Juicy, Gooey 9

Bartleby kept paddling toward streams of light. But every time he got close, the glittering patch of gnats seemed to disappear. He was soon exhausted. I'd better nap, he thought. A rest might help me swim faster.

This time it was easier to scramble up onto a broad, bobbing leaf. Bartleby rested quietly, letting the sun warm his carapace. He waited for the floating feeling to come, bringing colors, smells, and sounds.

Instead, a scratchy whine pricked his ears. It wasn't like the twins' fighting or Davy's crying. It stirred something else inside Bartleby. He felt a quick pulsing in his throat. His jaw tensed. His webs quivered. He twisted his neck this way and that, searching. At last, he saw it.

A plump green fly was hovering over a white flower. The fly dipped inside and flew out. Bartleby's hopes sank as it darted away.

But in another instant, the fly returned. Bartleby was silent. He felt the teeniest touch of a wing on his shell.

The fly doesn't know I'm me! he realized.

The fly flew back inside the flower. When it reappeared, its legs were coated with heavy, yellow dust. For a moment, it hovered above the flower. Then it flew slowly away, right toward Bartleby.

His jaws opened and snapped.

A tangy, salty sensation rolled across Bartleby's tongue. He could hardly believe how delicious the fly tasted. The legs were rough and crisp. When Bartleby bit down, they made the same crunchy sounds he'd heard when the boys ate potato chips. The wings were delicious, too! So light and thin, even more delicate than turtle flakes. Eagerly, Bartleby tried the head. He liked its chewy texture and the way his jaws had to work. Goo ran down his throat. He gulped and gulped until there wasn't a single bit of fly left.

Bartleby slipped off the lily pad and into the water. He wanted more! He drifted silently in the water, looking and listening, alert for a whisk or a ripple.

Before long his ears picked up a high-pitched hum. *Eeeeeeee.* "Food!" Bartleby whispered to himself. His jaws tensed, and his webs quivered.

The vibrations got faster and louder. Bartleby let his eyes close to a slit. In another moment he sighted a horribly ugly creature. It had a swollen red body and long, hairy legs. Just below its bulgy black eyes, a spiky tube protruded. Bartleby realized he knew the thing. It was a mosquito.

Davy and his brothers hated mosquitoes! Whenever

one flew in the house, they tried to swat it. Yet something inside Bartleby was making him crave this mosquito. He sank lower in the water and trailed it. The mosquito led him to the mud bank. Bartleby climbed out into the tall, feathery grass.

Suddenly, he heard a shrill voice cry:

> "Keep away from my eggs.
> I can kick, I've got legs!"

Bartleby halted. He pulled his head and limbs into his shell. "Wh-who's out there?" he stammered.

> "Don't try a trick,
> or I'll give you a kick!"

"I'm not trying anything," Bartleby responded. "I was just following a mosquito."

> "If this nest you come near,
> you have much to fear."

Was this one of the creatures that might swallow him? Bartleby was terrified. "I didn't mean to disturb your nest. I'll go away."

> "Yes, yes, go back,
> before I attack."

"All right, I'm leaving." Bartleby started to turn back—and stopped. As quietly as he could, he crawled to the edge of a little clearing and peeked between the blades of grass.

Bartleby had seen the nests of birds and squirrels in the trees outside his window. But he'd never seen a nest on the ground like this one. It was a large, roundish mound of dry grass, sticks, and mud. He wondered who it belonged to. The only creature in sight appeared to be a frog. Not the mean bigfrog at the lily patch, but a tiny, light brown one, even smaller than Bartleby. It was perched on the edge of the big nest.

"Perhaps the fierce creature is down inside," he told himself. He decided to see. "Excuse me, but I was wondering how many eggs you have?" he called.

The wee frog opened its mouth and cried:

"If these eggs you dare steal,
you will be my next meal!"

Bartleby blinked in amazement. He'd been fooled by a creature smaller than he was! He stuck his neck out farther and announced, "I am not trying to steal your eggs. And I am not afraid of you." He plodded to the thick, round nest and peered up at the little rhymer. "This big nest is yours?" he asked.

"It belongs to Mother Wak.
I'm on guard till she comes back."

"Mother Wak? Is she very fierce?" Bartleby stretched out his neck and looked from side to side.

"She's a dear mallard duck
who's had very bad luck!"

Bartleby eyed the frog more carefully. Its teeny legs were hardly big enough to kick a gnat away. It didn't appear to have a single tooth. It didn't even have a shell. "How can a creature as small as you guard this nest?" he asked.

"I am quite proud
for my peep is so loud.
If I call Mother Wak,
she'll come flying right back!"

The tiny creature hopped down in front of Bartleby. She had a dark, X-shaped marking on her back and a stubby little tail. "What are those lines on your back for?" he asked.

"I'm Zip of the peepers.
We're also good leapers.
That mark is a feature
of our kind of creature."

"Oh, like my ear bands." Bartleby turned his head from side to side so she could see his red patches. "I am

47

Bartleby, a red-eared turtle. My home is a great river," he said. To Bartleby's surprise, Zip leapt on his carapace.

> *"I like your shell.*
> *It fits you quite well.*
> *Can I come in, too,*
> *if I don't bother you?"*

"I'm afraid there's only room for one," Bartleby told her. But he liked the light, tickly feeling of her on his back. "Er, Zip, what are you guarding the nest from?"

> *"Wings, webs, or legs—*
> *the ones that eat eggs.*
> *Something got two,*
> *and the eggs' daddy, too!"*

Bartleby pulled his head in. "Something ate two eggs? And their father?" Atop his carapace, he felt Zip quiver.

> *"All through the night*
> *Father Wak tried to fight.*
> *When the beast finally fled,*
> *the poor mallard was dead."*

"How awful!" Bartleby whispered. "What kind of creature was it?"

"Claw, Paw, or Jaw—
I'm afraid no one saw.
But a rumor's been spread
of a new beast to dread,
a native Mississippian
forced to live among our kin."

"A native Mississippian!" Bartleby repeated. "Like me."

"There are many to fear.
Keep a watch out, Red-ear."

Bartleby heard a strange, muttering voice. Around him, the tall grass rustled and the air stirred. Something was approaching in a great hurry. What if it was the Claw, the Paw, and the Jaw? "Quick, hide!" he whispered to Zip. He tucked himself in tighter.

"*Wak-wak-wak!* I'm coming, Zip-*wak*! How are my six little egglets-*wak*?"

Zip began hopping up and down excitedly.

> "*It's Mother Wak!*
> *She's coming back.*"

Bartleby poked his head out just as a large bird came waddling into the clearing on wide webbed feet. She had a flat bill and feathers that were the soft, weathered shades of tree bark. Without noticing him, she went to the nest and looked inside.

"One-*wak*! Two-*wak*! Three-*wak*! Four-*wak*! Five-*wak*!

Six-*wak*!" she announced. "Thank you for keeping my egglets safe while I dabbled, Zip-*wak*! Oh, the shallows are filled with tender morsels for a duck's breakfast! *Wak-wak-wak*!" Carefully, she settled herself over her family.

For a moment, Bartleby was swept up by a powerful memory. He caught the pungent, slightly acrid smell of new life—the scent inside a turtle egg. He felt the warmth of being gently covered by mud and leaves. And then the memory was gone.

"I had some pleasant company—
this red-eared turtle, Bartleby."

"Bartleby-*wak*?" Mother Wak looked down her bill. "I've never seen a turtle with red ear bands before-*wak*!"

Bartleby edged his head out a bit. "I'm not exactly from around here. My family is from . . . " He hesitated a moment. But Mother Wak was staring at him with her bright, sharp eyes. "The Mighty Mississippi," Bartleby whispered.

"*Wak*! The Mississippi-*wak*! Claw, Paw, Jaw-*wak-wak-wak*!" The duck puffed up her feathers and spread her wings to cover her nest. She looked twice as big as before. And twice as frightening.

She's probably heard the rumor, Bartleby thought. Whatever the rumor was, it was the reason no one around this water place liked the Mighty Mississippi.

He began crawling back toward the water. He didn't

realize Zip was behind him until she hopped onto his shell again.

"Do you want to play a game?
It's lots of fun. Slip! is its name."

Bartleby stopped. He stretched his head up. "A game? Really, Zip?"

"Yes, it's time for us to have some fun,
now that our nest-sitting's done!
Good-bye for now, dear Mother Wak.
Do not worry, I'll be back."

When he'd lived with the boys, Bartleby had played many different games. He'd liked the one in which Davy let him walk all over the flat pieces that fit together to make a picture of a funny, hairy, human-looking creature. But he hadn't liked others. He wondered if he would like Zip's game.

"How do you play Slip?" he asked as they reached the water.

"On a lily pad you stay
while others make the water sway.
They swim and splash till you're so tippy
into the water you go slippy!"

"That sounds like fun!" Bartleby said, remembering how he'd slid off the lily pad the first time he'd tried to climb aboard. Suddenly, he thought of something else. "Zip, did you say that we are going to play with others?"

"Croakers and peepers,
crawlers and creepers.
The last one to remain
is champion of the game!"

Bartleby was so excited, he swallowed a mouthful of water. "Are any of the crawlers turtles?" he asked when he could speak again.

"Turtles often join in Slip!
It's not so hard to make them tip.
The bigfrogs are the ones to beat.
Watch out for Bully—he's a cheat!"

But Bartleby didn't care about the frogs. He couldn't wait to meet other turtles. He paddled behind Zip as she made her way through the water, always staying close to shore. After a while, they came to a place where a tree had fallen over onto the mud bank. One of its branches reached out into the water.

Bartleby stopped paddling and stared. Turtles! The branch was covered with them. The skin on their faces, legs, and tails was dark green with bright yellow stripes. Their carapaces were flat and round. Some rested their foreclaws or even their plastrons on their neighbors. All had their heads tilted toward the sun as they peacefully basked together.

Bartleby inspected the sides of their heads for red ear patches. Not a single turtle seemed to have them. Suddenly, he felt very shy. What if they didn't like him?

But Zip swam ahead without slowing down. She frog-kicked right up to the branch and announced:

> *"I've brought a creature here today,*
> *a turtle who would like to play.*
> *Who will challenge him to Slip!*
> *and try to make our new friend tip?"*

Slowly, the turtles turned their heads toward the place where Bartleby was quietly drifting. "What are the red things on the sides of your head?" the biggest one asked. He was nearly the size of a boy's foot.

Bartleby felt like tucking his head in. "They're ear patches. I'm a red-eared turtle."

"We are painted turtles. All of us." The big turtle blinked. "Where is your family?"

Bartleby thought for a moment. "They're, they're . . . far away."

"Faraway? Never heard of it." The big turtle turned its head up to the sun once again.

"I don't want to play with those snooty turtles any-way," Bartleby said to himself. He began paddling away, although he wasn't sure where he was going. He was be-ginning to miss Davy. At least the boy liked him.

"I'll play Slip!" a voice called.

Bartleby stopped. A small turtle tumbled off the log and swam toward him. "I'm Webster."

"Pleased to meet you," Bartleby said.

"Me, too!" called another, diving in next. "I'm Ripley."

"Wait for me!" called a third. "I'm Patience."

Playmates! Turtle playmates! Bartleby was so full of happiness, he felt as if he might burst out of his shell.

A tiny frog that looked a lot like Zip sprang off the mud bank.

"Can the game include one other?
I'm Hopalot, Zip's closest brother!"

"Zip, I didn't know you had a brother," Bartleby said. "Are there more in your family?"

"I once had a thousand, two hundred and nine,
Hoppy's egg sac was the one next to mine.
Now that we have enough creatures to play,
off to the lily pads—I'll lead the way!"

Slip!

11

The teams for Slip! were set to play. The two leadoff players, Bartleby and Webster, were hunkered down on lily pads, facing each other. At the count of three, Ripley and Hoppy began swimming around Bartleby, trying to stir up the water and jiggle him off the leaf. Zip and Patience did the same around Webster. All swimmers chanted as they circled the lily pads:

"Slip and Slide! Slide and Slip!
Now it's time to take a dip!"

Bartleby observed how Webster flattened his webs against the pad to make them wide, and how he sometimes saved himself from tipping over by using his tail. He tried to copy Webster, but the sloshing water was making his lily pad quite slippery.

"Keep toward the center of the leaf," a familiar voice advised. Bartleby looked up and saw a flash of bright blue wing. The kingfisher was watching the game from his branch.

There was a loud splash as something fat and fast leapt into the water. Bartleby's leaf began rocking. He slid all the way to the edge. Just in the nick of time, he pushed out his foreclaws and managed to stop.

A big, widemouthed head popped up in the water beside him—Bully's head. "Let's play frogs against turtles!" the bigfrog croaked.

"B-but I'm already in a game," Bartleby said, backing toward the center of his lily pad again.

"That game's over," Bully informed him. He opened his mouth and called, *"Rrroak! Rrroak!"* Two bigfrogs popped up in front of Webster's lily pad. One of the frogs reached out a leg and pushed Webster into the water.

"Hey!" Webster exclaimed. "No fair!"

"That's right, no touching," the kingfisher agreed.

"Why don't you mind your own business, fish-slapper!" Bully bellowed. With two strong kicks, he swam over to Webster's lily pad and hopped on it himself. "Frogs against turtles!" he ordered.

But Zip and Hopalot swam over to Bartleby's lily pad.

*"Hoppy and I would rather be
on a team with Bartleby!"*

"Go ahead. Peepers aren't real frogs, anyway," Bully replied.

"They're just as real as you are, Bully! And I'd be glad to have them on my team." Bartleby was amazed to hear himself speak so boldly.

"Ripley, Patience, and I will play on Bartleby's team, too," Webster said.

Bully puffed out his chest. "Three of us and six of you. That should even things out. Come on! You're wasting my time."

Together, Bartleby's teammates tried to stir up the water around Bully. They dove down and popped up. They splashed their webs. The three turtles used their tails to churn the surface while Zip and Hoppy blew bubbles.

The two bigfrogs leapt in and out of the water making splashy explosions all around Bartleby. One side of Bartleby's lily pad rocked up so high, he was nearly spilled off. By scrambling to the far edge, he managed to right it again.

"Excellent recovery," the kingfisher called.

"Thank you!" Bartleby replied. This balancing game was the most fun he'd ever had. He rode the lily pad as it bobbed and swirled.

But soon, Bartleby began to tire. He backed up toward the center of his leaf and pulled in his limbs. He squinched his eyes halfway shut and thought of balancing.

Bully was tiring, too. Even though the turtles and peepers were small creatures, they'd managed to keep his lily pad tipping this way and that. "I've had enough," he grumbled. "I give up." He crouched down as if he were about to dive into the water. Instead, he stretched out one of his big legs, sneaked a webbed foot under Bartleby's leaf—and kicked it over.

"That's cheating," the kingfisher scolded.

"That's winning!" Bully croaked, hopping to a lily pad at the far edge of the patch.

Bartleby paddled out from under his upturned leaf. He thought about tipping Bully into the water. But he wasn't sure he was strong enough. Instead, he just glared at the cheating bigfrog—and saw something peculiar.

Bully was having trouble staying upright on the lily pad. It seemed to be moving by itself. But it wasn't rocking or swaying or bobbing. It was rising straight up in the air!

"That is no lily pad," Bartleby said to himself as a long, narrow head emerged under Bully. The head had hard black eyes and rough green skin.

"Bully, jump!" Bartleby shouted. "Swim away! Hurry!"

Ssseezer

12

Bully sprang and vanished like a raindrop in a puddle. The long-headed creature whipped itself around toward the splash. "If I wanted to, I could catch him easily. I could ssswallow him up in a sssnap," it said. "I could have caught any one of your friends. But I didn't feel like it."

"That's good," Bartleby managed to say.

He glanced from side to side. Zip, Hoppy, the bigfrogs, and the turtles had disappeared so quietly he hadn't even heard them. He wanted to swim away, too, but his limbs were stiff with fear.

"Perhaps not ssso good for you." The creature glided closer. Its long, flat tail swept back and forth in the water as it moved. "Do you know why I didn't eat that fat, sssilly bullfrog?"

Bartleby back-paddled a bit. "Because he might've stuck in your throat and choked you?" He was pretty sure it could happen. This creature was quite skinny, even though it was nearly as long as a baseball bat.

The long, flat tail struck the water. "Not at all! It is because I sssmelled sssomething better—the sssalty, sssilty ssscent of prey from home. We had many ssscrumptious red-ears near my nest on the Mississippi."

Prey? Bartleby thought he knew what *prey* meant. Above Bartleby's plastron, his heart was fluttering like a gnat's wings. "You're from the Mighty Mississippi?"

The creature rose up higher in the water so Bartleby could see more of its thick, bumpy hide. "Sssertainly. I am Ssseezer of the Mighty Mississippi. Don't you recognize me?"

"Are you the Claw, the Paw, and the Jaw?" Bartleby whispered.

"I sssuppose I could be. I am an alligator and your enemy. Are you sssertain you don't know me?"

"An alligator? I don't think so," Bartleby replied. "Although my family may be from the Mighty Mississippi, I've been a pet. I am really only Bartleby of the Bowl." Bartleby eyed the creature's long, toothy jaws and flat tail. Suddenly he remembered something. "My boy had a plaything that looked like you!" he exclaimed.

"A plaything?" Ssseezer snorted so hard, he practically blew Bartleby out of the water.

"If you're from the Mighty Mississippi, what are you doing here?" Bartleby asked. He back-paddled toward a lily pad, hoping the alligator wouldn't notice.

"I was kidnapped! Sssnared in a net while I was ssstill

61

just a hatchling." Ssseezer sank down in the water. "I've been a pet, too."

"You!" Behind him, Bartleby could feel a lily pad with his web. If only the alligator would look away, he could duck under it.

"Yesss. I had a little girl. Ssshe kept me in a tank and fed me crickets and worms. One time, when I was es-sspecially hungry, I mistook her finger for a worm and bit it. That made her cry. The very next day her father brought me to this water place. 'Look out, all you pond creatures! Here comesss Seezer of the Mississippi,' he yelled. Then he left me."

Bartleby gulped. "He left you here forever? My boy will be back for me. At least, he said he would." If only Davy would appear right now! Bartleby thought.

"Good riddance, I sssay! Every day I am growing and gaining ssstrength ssso I can return home. I just need to learn the way."

The water rippled. Ssseezer had disappeared. Bartleby glanced around. Where had he gone?

The alligator surfaced, snout to snout with Bartleby. "You may have been a pet, but your ssscent is the ssscent of Mississippi water. I wonder if your taste is the taste of the Mississippi, too?"

Bartleby stared down the creature's long, open jaws. There was a dark, terrifying cave just where his teeth ended. In another moment, Bartleby thought, he might be in there. Forever. "Maybe I could help you find the way back to the Mighty Mississippi," he whispered.

The long jaws jabbed at Bartleby. "What! You know the way?"

Bartleby didn't want to lie. Neither did he want to be eaten. "N-not exactly. But I think I might have seen something in one of my naps. If I tried, I might remember."

"Yes, remember, little Red-ear. That would be very useful." Seezer inhaled so deeply, Bartleby was nearly sucked into his mouth. "Ahhh, the sssweet ssscent of water lilies always makes me sssleepy." He closed his jaws. "All right, Bartleby. I will go back to my den and nap now. But I'll sssee you again sssoon. Perhaps by then, you will have remembered the way home."

Exhausted and fearful, Bartleby pulled himself onto a lily pad. The twins were right, he thought. He was dumb. He'd been here only one day, and already he'd almost been eaten. Maybe life had been boring in his bowl, but at least he'd been safe. He was beginning to wish he'd never heard of the Mighty Mississippi.

"You don't really know the way back to the river, do you?"

Bartleby recognized the rough voice of the kingfisher bird. He looked up. "No, I don't," he admitted.

"That's too bad," the kingfisher sympathized. "I guess you're in trouble."

"*Rrroak!* We're all in trouble!" Bully's head popped up between two lily leaves. "If that alligator creature stays

63

here much longer, he's going to get bigger. And he's going to need a lot to eat! Including those minnows you like, Kingfisher."

"My lilies!" the muskrat squeaked. " 'E likes to zmell my lilies. 'E better not like to eeet my lilies!"

Webster clambered up beside Bartleby. "One thing is certain. From now on, we'd all better be extra careful." He bumped his shell gently against Bartleby's. "Especially you."

Bartleby felt something leap onto his carapace. Terrified, he pulled his head in. But it was only Zip.

"You were awfully brave and tough
to face a beast so very gruff."

"I'm not brave, Zip," Bartleby protested, edging his head out. "I just didn't know how to escape." But the peeper didn't seem to hear him.

"I fear that 'gator is so bad,
he ate the egglets and their dad.
Please recall the route, Red-ear,
so we can send him far from here!"

"Oh, Zip," Bartleby moaned. "I don't know how to get to the Mississippi. I've only seen flashes of rushing water in my naps. I don't even know if it's the mighty river at all."

The Claw, the Paw, and the Jaw

13

When his new friends were gone, Bartleby scanned the water, hoping for a glimpse of Mudly's white-striped head. "Mudly is wise," he said to himself. "Perhaps he knows how to find the Mighty Mississippi."

But from the shallows, all Bartleby could see was the gray, sloped back of a very large animal. It seemed to be standing in the middle of the big water. Bartleby paddled toward it. To his surprise, Mudly was sitting on the animal's humped back. But the stinkpot didn't seem to be afraid. In fact, his head was stretched up toward the sun as if he were enjoying himself.

"Perhaps Mudly is just sitting on the great creature's back the way Zip sat on my shell," Bartleby said to himself. "Perhaps the great creature is even protecting Mudly." He gathered his courage and headed into the deeper water.

It was a tiring swim. When he was only a few strokes

away, he saw it wasn't a creature's back at all. It was a rock—the biggest, most beautiful rock Bartleby had ever seen. It seemed to grow out of the water the way a tree grew from the earth. Its solid, gray surface was flecked with sparkles. When he touched it with a forefoot, it felt warm and alive.

"Mudly, may I join you?" Bartleby called.

"Come on up," the stinkpot replied. "Basking is good for the appetite. The more you eat, the more you grow. The more you grow, the harder you are to swallow."

With his sharp nails, Bartleby grasped the grainy surface, pulling and pushing until he felt gentle heat through his plastron.

Mudly turned his head toward Bartleby. "Congratulations. You found the best place in the pond for basking and napping."

Napping! Bartleby didn't think he could ever go to sleep again. "Can't we talk first? I have so much to tell you."

"What?" Mudly's eyes began to close.

"I met a terrifying beast!"

Mudly's eyes shut.

"A creature from the Mighty Mississippi."

Mudly's eyes opened again. "The rumor! Then it's true! Why didn't you say so?"

"I am saying so!" Bartleby edged farther up the rock. "He's an alligator. His name is Seezer."

Mudly blinked. He opened his mouth, but he didn't utter a sound.

"Seezer wants to go back to his home in the Mighty Mississippi, but he doesn't know how to get there. I told him I might know the way—but I only said that so he wouldn't eat me. Do you know the way?"

Mudly let out a long sigh. "I've never been beyond this water. My family and my family's family never went beyond this water. But if you sleep, you might find the way."

"Sleep! How can I find the way if I'm sleeping?"

"Sleep . . ." Mudly's eyes were closing.

It was quiet and comfortable on the basking rock. A gentle breeze caressed Bartleby's snout. Suddenly, he was exhausted. "Mudly," he said as he lowered himself onto his plastron, "who is the Claw, the Paw, and the Jaw? Is it Seezer?"

"Mmmm, he's one." Mudly's eyes were shut. "Later, we will talk. . . ."

One? Did Mudly mean that there were other alligators in their water? Bartleby wanted to know right now! But the floaty feeling was starting. He tried his best to resist it. "Mudly, how many of the Claw, the Paw, and the Jaw are there?" he whispered.

But Mudly was deep inside a turtle nap. In another moment, Bartleby was, too.

The air was cooler when Bartleby awoke. He tried to recapture his dream. He could remember noisy, churning

67

water and the giddy feeling of being swept along. Had it been the Mighty Mississippi?

All of a sudden, he felt a great emptiness inside. He had to eat before he could think about the river—or anything. "Mudly, I'm starved!" he said, recalling the tangy taste of his breakfast fly. "Let's hunt."

Mudly raised his head. "Mmm, yes! I dreamed of chewing something fat and gushy. Perhaps I'll find it now."

They slid off the basking rock into the soft, refreshing water. Mudly swam ahead with strong, swift strokes. Bartleby followed at his beginner's pace, but he didn't mind. Everywhere he looked, new creatures were swimming or flying. Shimmery four-winged flies zipped overhead. Spidery-legged insects skittered on top of the water. Swarms of three-tailed worms wriggled and scattered as Bartleby paddled through them. And once, a shiny black beetle nearly as big as Bartleby eyed him and smacked its jaws.

A series of slow vibrations tickled his plastron. Bartleby peered down and saw the gray, curved shapes of fish drifting quietly beneath him. Next, a shimmer of silver attracted his attention. A school of tiny, slender fish hovered in the shadow of a water plant. The fish gazed at Bartleby with blank, staring eyes. "Boo!" he shouted, and they darted away. The silly fish made him glad to be a turtle, even if he was a small, inexperienced one.

When Mudly stopped to snap up water fleas, Bartleby

caught up to him. "You said you would tell me about the Paw, the Claw, and the Jaw," he reminded the stinkpot. "Are there more alligators?"

"Alligators? I don't believe so," Mudly mumbled with his mouth full of flea. "But the Claw, the Paw, and the Jaw are many creatures. Some are fierce and powerful. Some are quick and cunning. And some are skillful hunters and ceaseless eaters."

Even though the afternoon was warm, Bartleby felt himself shiver. "Like alligators," he murmured.

"Yes, I suppose so."

"Who else?"

"Birds. Raccoons. Skunks. Foxes. I am sorry to say even our own cousin, *Chelydra serpentina*, the snapping turtle, hunts its relatives."

Bartleby looked up. He searched the mud bank. He scanned the water. The Jaw, the Paw, and the Claw are everywhere, he thought. He eyed a bit of yellowish-green leech hanging out of the stinkpot's jaw. "Mudly, are you one of them, too?"

Mudly stopped chomping and blinked. "In a way, I guess I am—and so are you. All of us are the Claw, the Paw, and the Jaw to the creatures we eat."

"Even me!" Bartleby stretched out his neck and held up his head. "I am the Claw, the Paw, and the Jaw," he murmured to himself. He snapped his jaws as loudly as he could.

When Mudly started paddling again, Bartleby tried to follow. But he'd taken only a few strokes when, faster than a fly could flit, his companion disappeared underwater. Only the putrid scent of stinkpot remained in the air.

Friend

14

Bartleby stuck his head beneath the surface, but he didn't follow Mudly. The tangled plants and dim light underwater made it hard to see—and he wasn't sure what was down there.

"Mudly?" he called softly.

A moment later, his friend's striped head popped up. In his jaws, Mudly held a small object that looked like a swirly stone. *Crunch!* As Bartleby watched in amazement, Mudly bit down and cracked the stone. A black strand oozed from the stinkpot's jaws.

"Snail," Mudly said when he could speak again. "They grow plump and chewy on the muck at the bottom."

Bartleby felt his middle tighten hungrily. "Is it far to the bottom?"

"In some places. The deepest part is in the center. That's where I like to hunt and sleep." Mudly slurped the gummy thing down his throat. "Delicious! I think I'll dive down for another. Come on! There's more than enough for both of us."

Bartleby looked into the water again. He thought he saw a dark shape moving below. "I'm not that hungry after all. I think I'll just swim to the lily pads and catch a few flies. I want to practice playing Slip! while it's still light."

"Pleasant eating, then," Mudly replied. He dove under the water.

Bartleby paddled in and out of the lily pads. There were plenty of mayflies and gnats to eat. Every few strokes, he dipped his head under the water and looked down. All he could see was a forest of long, thick stems. Once he took a few strokes downward, but a tendril-like thing brushed his face, and he practically leapt out of the water like Bully.

He heard some buzzing and croaking, but he couldn't see anyone to play with. He climbed onto a leaf and crawled around the edges, trying to make it tippy. He pulled in his limbs and rolled back and forth by pushing from side to side with his tail. As he began to feel braver, he let himself slip headfirst into the water. But each time, he stayed under only for a moment before he paddled up again.

As the sun sank in the sky, Bartleby grew tired. He chose a sturdy pad with a large blossom beside it and climbed on. Then he waited for the floaty feeling to come.

The flash of colors was just beginning when he felt something poke the underside of the lily pad. Bartleby's eyes popped open. "Perhaps someone has come to play Slip! with me," he said, trying to calm himself. He pulled his head and limbs in and waited. And felt another poke. The leaf began to bob.

With his tail, Bartleby stopped himself from sliding off. He thought about crawling to the center of the leaf, where he could be more stable. But he decided to keep still. He slowed his breathing to the gentle rhythm of the rocking leaf. For a few moments, all was calm and silent, as if everyone were hiding.

Something nudged the pad again, right under his plastron. Before he could stop himself, Bartleby called out, "Bully? Webster? Is this a game?"

"It could be a game if you'd like, friend," a voice replied, low and rolling.

Bartleby didn't recognize the voice. He clamped his mouth shut to keep from answering.

"Aren't you lonely here by yourself, friend? Don't you want to play?"

Could it really be a friend? Bartleby peeked out. The sun had set, and the moon was beginning to rise. In its whitish light he could see something floating nearby. It looked like a long, narrow tail with small black eyes and a slit for a mouth. It flowed toward Bartleby like water on water.

Bartleby felt a pinging of alarm. He jerked his head in and willed the thing to go away.

"Come now, friend, why not be friendly? I could show you some very useful moves."

"I d-don't think we are f-friends," Bartleby stammered. "We've never even m-met."

A skinny tongue darted in and out of the thing's mouth. "We could be friends. While we play, we can get to know each other."

The creature's slow, slithery movements were so scary, Bartleby could hardly speak. "I think I know enough about you already," Bartleby replied without poking his head out. "And I don't want to play with you."

"But it's not fair, friend! No one ever wants to play with me! And I could be such a good player, too. So quick. So flexible. So powerful . . ."

"I don't really think you want to play at all. I think you want to eat me." Bartleby was quivering so hard, he was making the leaf bob.

"Oh, I do want to play—really! It's just that whenever I'm with friends, I can't help some things. I can't help wanting to be even closer friends. Inseparable friends. Friends to the end . . ." The creature flowed forward.

Bartleby scrunched up in his shell as tight as he could. He closed his eyes and waited. Suddenly, a shrill voice filled the air.

"Creatures awake! Beware of the snake!
It's Bartleby he's trying to take.

"Creatures arise! Behold with your eyes!
He calls himself Friend, but his tongue always lies!"

"Zip!" Bartleby whispered to himself. "She must be here among the lily pads." He opened his eyes to look for her—and saw the snake's jaws, open and ready to snap. Without thinking, he stuck out his limbs and began scrabbling backward.

Whoosh! Something—someone—grabbed one of his hind webs and pulled him down under the water.

Surprises Under the Water

15

Bartleby struggled to free himself. Something had a very tight grip on his right rear web. It was dragging him backward through the water—not deep, but just underneath the lily-pad patch. He tried to see what it was, but he couldn't turn around.

In another moment, he was yanked into a tunnel, a black, twisty passageway that was filled with water. Bartleby could feel thick, solid mud walls as he was pulled through the zigzagging maze.

And then he was tugged upward, out of the water and into a dim, roomy den. He could feel dried grass under his webs. All he could see was a small, shadowy mound in a corner. Whoever had been pulling him let go now.

"That snake almost eeet you," a voice said.

"Muskrat!" Bartleby gasped. "Where are we?"

"My 'ouse." Muskrat sat up on his hind legs and

snatched something off the pile in the corner. Eagerly, he began gnawing with his long front teeth.

"What's that?" Bartleby asked.

"My lovely, lovely lily roots." Muskrat paused for a long moment. "You want any?"

"No. I'm too tired to eat anything."

Even in the dark, Bartleby could see Muskrat's eyes brighten at his answer. "Good, good. You nap. In the morning, you go out the top."

"The top?" Bartleby looked up.

Muskrat sniffed proudly. "I made many tunnels. In through water, out on mud bank." He pointed his nose up toward an overhead tunnel.

"That's the way out?" Bartleby asked, craning his neck up.

"Shhh!" Muskrat said, although they seemed to be alone. "It's 'idden. Big pile of grass and leaves over opening."

"Don't worry," Bartleby said. "I won't tell." He settled down into the soft straw floor. "Muskrat, thank you. I'm really glad you came along!"

"Got to take care of you, red-ear. You're going to send the long-jaw far away from my lilies."

Bartleby awoke, yearning for sunlight and fresh air. Even though it was very dark, his hunger told him it was morning. He squinted his eyes and looked around. In the corner, Muskrat was asleep on top of his pile of lily roots.

"Muskrat, I think I'll leave now," Bartleby said.

Muskrat didn't stir.

Bartleby knew he could go back down through the water. But he was afraid to return to the dark, twisty tunnel again. To reach the overhead passage he tried scrabbling up the side of the mud wall. It was too steep.

"Muskrat, could you give me a boost up?" he finally asked.

The furry creature just wrapped his scaly tail tighter around himself and sighed.

"I'll have to climb on him. I hope he won't mind," Bartleby said to himself. He plodded over and began pulling himself up the mound of roots. Then he grabbed hold of Muskrat's thick coat. There was a mumble—but Muskrat stayed asleep. Bartleby clambered up, grasping the dampish fur with sharp little foreclaws. The sweet scent of lilies wafted from the fur as he climbed. From the highest point on Muskrat's back, Bartleby could just reach the hole overhead.

"Good-bye, friend," he whispered, and pulled himself out.

He found Mudly hunting fish fry in the warm, shallow water. "Chase them into the water grass. It will slow them down and make them easier to catch," the stinkpot advised.

Soon Bartleby's insides were stuffed with the delicious little creatures. He couldn't eat a bite more, but he paddled after them anyway, enjoying the hunt—around a clump of feathery stalks, under a tangle of floating twigs, over a slick patch of moldy leaves. Sometimes, when he got very close, the tiny fish leapt out of the water to evade him. Other times, he sank down and floated, silently waiting. Soon, thinking he was a leaf, an unsuspecting fishling would settle over his carapace. What fun it was to begin paddling and surprise the creature!

"Time to sun and nap!" Mudly called. "The basking rock will be delightfully warm now."

But Bartleby wasn't ready to rest. He wanted to swim more—and play! "I'll join you later," he told the stinkpot. Eagerly, he began paddling toward the fallen tree beyond the lily-pad patch. He could see the line of painted turtles already basking. Perhaps Webster, Patience, and Ripley would want to join in a game of Slip!

Ahead, on the water's surface, there were bubbles. Shimmery, jiggly, light-filled balls. They were so pretty, Bartleby drifted in for a closer look. Another bubble rose up. And another!

And then a pair of nostrils—and a wide, flat snout. "Ah, Bartleby! I thought I sssmelled the delicious ssscent of the Mississippi. Oh, how you make me miss my bayou!"

One by one, the sparkling bubbles popped and vanished. Bartleby wished he could vanish, too. There was

nowhere for him to go. Seezer was circling him—
enclosing him as tightly as if he were in a bowl.

"What's a b-bayou?" Bartleby asked, hoping to distract the alligator.

Seezer's eyes sparkled. "A ssswampy inlet filled with
sssweet river water. Perfect for an alligator's nest! The
air always ssstank of rotting leaves and carcasses my
mother buried in our burrow. Delightful!"

"Is bayou water warm and muddy?" Bartleby quickly
asked. At least while he's talking, he can't be eating,
Bartleby thought.

"Oh, yes," Seezer replied in a dreamy voice. "The
sssurface is covered with the yummiest mosquito and flea
eggs."

"It sounds like a perfect home for you. Much better
than this water place." Bartleby had to paddle in circles
to keep his eyes on the alligator. It was making him dizzy.

"Perfect? Not at all!" Seezer thundered. "When we
youngsters ssswam, fish with mouths like caves would
chase us. Raccoons pawed through the ssshallows trying
to grab us! Birds ssswooped down and tried to sssnatch
us! One of them ate my favorite brother, Al. Oh, how I
despise web-footed birds! If I ever get the chance, I will
pay them back!"

"B-but you're bigger now," Bartleby whispered. "They
would never try to harm you. Besides, your brother could
have been eaten by another creature. One of those raccoons you mentioned—or a snake."

"There were duck prints in the mud. I sssaw them with my own eyes!" Seezer slapped his tail, raining water on Bartleby's shell.

"T-tell me more about your bayou," Bartleby whispered, hoping to calm him.

"Everywhere, there were rotting ssstumps to bask upon," Seezer said. "And chirping crickets to lull me to ssssleep." He stopped circling and sank down in the water. "I haven't had a decent night's ssslumber sssince I was brought to New York."

New York? Is that where we are? Bartleby wondered. How would he ever learn the way to Seezer's bayou if he didn't even know where he was now? "Is New York far from the Mississippi?" he asked.

"How ssshould I know? You sssaid you knew the way!" Seezer bellowed.

Bartleby tucked his head in. "When I nap, I sometimes have memories. Rushing, churning water that is hurrying somewhere. But my naps are mysterious. I don't yet know where the water goes. Or where it begins."

Seezer swam closer to him. So close, he could snap Bartleby up in an instant. "Turtles may be ssslow and ssssteady, but alligators are fast and hasty. I will go sssmell the lilies to calm myself. But you had better dream of the way back home, Bartleby. Before I lose my patience."

Terrified, Bartleby watched the V-shaped trail the alligator left in the water as he swam toward the lily patch. Bartleby hoped none of his friends were hiding there.

A small striped head popped up nearby. "Bartleby! Are you all right?" Webster called. "I was sure that awful beast would eat you!"

"He *is* going to eat me if I'm not able to tell him the way to the Mighty Mississippi soon."

"I wish I could help you," Webster said. "But my naps are only of sticky mud and still water." He began swimming toward the log where his family was basking. "Come on! When the others awake, we can ask them if they know the way. Perhaps one of them has heard something. Then we can play Slip!"

Little Green Egglet

16

When the sun began to sink, Bartleby returned to the grass that grew on the banks of the big water. He was hoping to find a safe spot where he could spend the night—a place where there were no snakes and no alligators. As quietly as he could, he pushed into a thick tuft of reeds. But he couldn't keep the tall, stiff blades from rustling.

"Wak-wak-wak!" a voice called in the darkness. "Keep away, fox-wak!"

In spite of his worry, Bartleby's spirits lifted. "I'm not a fox-wak," he called back. "It's me, Mother Wak—Bartleby."

"Bartleby-wak? The red-ear? Why aren't you asleep-wak?"

Bartleby followed her wakking through the grass until he reached the nest.

"Night is for sleeping, Bartleby-wak!" the mother duck

scolded. "You should be hidden away while the fierce ones are on the prowl."

"Oh, Mother Wak, I am very tired. But I don't know where to hide"—Bartleby lowered his voice—"from the Claw, the Paw, and the Jaw." He looked from side to side. Then he whispered, "Especially the alligator from the Mighty Mississippi."

"Wak-wak-wak!" Mother Wak puffed out her feathers. "I've seen his claw prints in the mud bank. I've seen the line his tail draws as he hunts. That creature cannot be trusted!"

"Are the egglets all right?" Bartleby asked.

"See for yourself." Mother Wak raised her rear end. Bartleby stood on his rear webs and peeked underneath.

Six eggs were nestled in a layer of soft duck feathers plucked from Mother Wak's own breast. The smooth tan shells were the same size as Bartleby.

"They look quite cozy and safe," he said wistfully.

"Yes-wak." Mother Wak sat back down and began preening her feathers. Suddenly she looked up again. "Would you like to sleep in the nest, Bartleby-wak? There's room near the back."

Something told Bartleby turtles didn't sleep under ducks' bottoms. What would Mudly say? But Bartleby was awfully tired. Beneath the duck he could be safe for a while.

He reached out a forefoot to pull himself up the side of the nest. His front webs groped soft feathers. "I'll be very careful," he promised. "I'll keep perfectly still and quiet."

It was soft and warm under Mother Wak's body. Pressed up against an egglet, Bartleby heard the ticking of a tiny heartbeat.

"Wak-wak! Bartleby-*wak*! Breakfast time!" Mother Wak rose to count her eggs.

Bartleby poked his head out. The sun was not yet up, and the sky was the gray white of earliest morning. "Who will watch the egglets while you're having breakfast?" he asked sleepily.

The duck ruffled her feathers and shook her rear end. "Since Father Wak died, I don't eat very often. But sometimes Zip-*wak* comes to watch the egglets. Then I dabble quickly—*wak!*—for whatever is nearby. At this time of year, there are many tender water plants in the shallows."

"I can stay in the nest and protect the eggs," Bartleby offered.

"You-*wak*? How can a little turtle like you protect the egglets-*wak*?"

Bartleby closed his eyes to think. "I'm not sure," he admitted. "But so far I've met a snake and an alligator, and I've survived. If the time comes, I may think of something." Gently, he smoothed a bit of grass over an egg with his snout. "Besides, you must eat so you will be strong enough to care for the eggs."

Mother Wak poked her head into the nest and rolled the egglets closer together. Bartleby marveled at how gentle she could be with her hard, wide beak. "All right, Bartleby-*wak*! I will leave you in charge of the nest while I eat. I'll be back as soon as I can. *Wak-wak-wak!*" She waddled off toward the big water.

Inside the nest, Bartleby kept his eyes wide open. He listened carefully to the noises from the woods. He heard squirrels chattering and birds calling. He felt a breeze across his carapace. This cool air might chill the eggs, he thought. He began pulling fluff from the side of the nest to cover them.

His mouth was full of duck down when something bounced off his shell. Startled, Bartleby jerked his head and limbs in.

> *"Did I surprise you, Bartleby,*
> *the same way that you startled me?*
> *I came to watch the egglets' nest*
> *and give poor Mother Wak a rest.*
> *Instead I found a red-eared friend*
> *on whom the egglets can depend."*

"Zip!" Bartleby poked his head out. "I am so glad to see you!"

The little peeper hopped up and down on Bartleby's carapace. The patting of her tiny feet felt as delicate as raindrops.

"Hop and I were chasing gnats
in and out the lily patch.
Suddenly, I had a scare—
the egglet thief was hiding there!"

"Do you mean Seezer?" Bartleby asked. "We don't know for certain that he's the one who ate the eggs. He says he comes to smell the lilies because they calm him."

"Smelling a lily?
Don't be so silly!
A 'gator that traps you
will lie as he snaps you!"

"Perhaps you are right," Bartleby agreed, remembering how much Seezer hated web-footed birds. Suddenly, the ground began to tremble. "Did you feel that?" he whispered. But Zip had already leapt out of the nest and disappeared into the grass.

"Who is there?" Bartleby called.

The sky above him darkened. Bartleby looked up. A furry face with two masked eyes stared down at him.

"Y-you're not Mother Wak," he stammered.

"You're not an egg," the masked creature replied.

Bartleby stretched out his neck as far as he could. "I am Bartleby of the Mighty Mississippi, a great fast river."

"I am a raccoon from the woods. A raccoon hungry for eggs. Now get away from my breakfast."

"But they belong to Mother Wak!"

"Finders, keepers," the raccoon said. She reached into the nest with a paw. Bartleby was surprised to see that it looked almost like a boy's hand.

"Wait!" he cried. Somehow he had to get this beast away from the nest. An idea came to him, but it was a dangerous one. Still, he couldn't let Mother Wak down without trying.

"Wouldn't you rather eat a tasty turtle instead?" Bartleby asked.

The raccoon cocked her head. "A turtle? Why would I eat you? Your shell is hard, and your skin is tough."

"Turtle meat is very tasty. Besides, I'm a rare turtle. A red-ear." Bartleby turned his head from side to side to display his bands. "No one around here has ever eaten red-ear before."

The raccoon's black eyes sparkled. With her long, curved nails, she stroked Bartleby's carapace. "Well, I suppose I could give you a try." She plucked him up and squeezed him in her paw. "But I'll have to wash you first. We raccoons are quite fussy."

Bartleby pulled his limbs into his shell. "You'd better hurry before my boys catch you," he said as the raccoon carried him toward the big water.

The raccoon stopped. "Boys? You have boys?"

"Three of them. I was their pet. They'll be back for me anytime now."

The raccoon loosened her grip a bit. She looked back over her shoulder. "Boys are bad."

"My boys were pretty bad," Bartleby agreed. "And they loved thick, soft raccoon fur like yours." He shut his mouth as the paw dipped him into the water. He stuck out his webs and tried to swim away, but the fingerlike claws were holding him too tightly.

"If you were a pet, how did you get here?" The raccoon lifted Bartleby toward her open mouth. He could see the whiskers on her nose quivering. He could feel her moist breath.

"I escaped," he said quickly. "I've been trying to hide from them ever since. But I'm afraid boys are very good hunters—especially my boys."

"I'm very good at escaping," the raccoon said, but her paw shook.

"Shh! Listen!" he said. "I think I hear them coming now."

The raccoon froze. Her paw twitched open. Bartleby felt himself drop into the water.

Without thinking about it, he dove for the bottom, pulling with all his might. He passed big, slow-moving fish and small, darting ones. Wavy plant stalks reached out for him. Forests of tangled roots nearly trapped him. The deeper he went, the harder it was to see. The colors of plants and rocks became dull and eerie.

"Everything looks different down here," he said aloud,

but his voice sounded so slow and drawn out, he scared himself. With a start, he realized that even the way he breathed had changed. He wasn't using his nostrils or mouth anymore, but he was still getting air. It seemed to be coming through his skin.

He pulled hard. Even though he was tired, he had to keep going. What if the raccoon was following him?

Finally, he reached the bottom of the big water. It was soft and thick and wonderfully slimy! Bartleby couldn't resist digging his forefeet in it. The squishy muck sucked at his claws. Delighted, he pushed his snout in, too. The lovely ooze felt gentle against his face. It made his head pleasantly muzzy. Bartleby pressed himself down farther. He dug with his forefeet. He kicked with his back feet. He closed his eyes and let himself sink through dark, rich mush until he was completely covered in it. He felt as if he were a hatchling in an egg again. And then he remembered.

"The eggs! I must return to Mother Wak's nest!" But his webs didn't move. The floaty feeling had already started in his head.

I'll just rest here for a moment, he thought. And then I'll go.

Five

17

At first there was only a sense of heading somewhere. Later, flashes of bubbly foam appeared, and the drifting became flowing. Bartleby felt himself rising, falling, and spinning. The flowing surged and roared and made Bartleby's insides pump wildly. But he wasn't afraid. He was thrilled.

He opened his eyes in squooshy slime. "Where am I?" he murmured. He poked his head up and found himself deep underwater. He tried to think, but his head was still muzzy. With his forefeet, he wiped the muck from his eyes and recognized the bottom of the big water place.

"It was only a dream," he said slowly. He began digging himself out of the mushy bottom, but his limbs seemed heavy and clumsy. He flapped his webs and moved his head and tail.

"The eggs!" he exclaimed as the groggy feeling finally vanished. His gasp sent a stream of bubbles floating upward. Bartleby followed them. As he approached the surface, he could see light. How long had be been asleep? he wondered. Was it day or night when he had left them?

He struggled to swim more quickly, angry at his small, weak webs. At last, he could see the surface glittering above him, and beyond it, a calm, blue sky. With a final spurt of energy, Bartleby burst through the water and began paddling toward the shore.

As fast as he could, he pulled himself up the mud bank. Mudly was there digging for worms. "Where have you been?" the stinkpot asked. "I've been looking for you all morning."

"I hid in the bottom to escape a raccoon," Bartleby said. "I only meant to stay a moment, but I slipped into a deep sleep."

"Bottom slime has that effect," Mudly said. "That is why we turtles like to rest there. There is no better place for a nap."

"But I was supposed to protect Mother Wak's eggs," Bartleby moaned. Above his plastron, his heart was beating fast. If only his legs could move with such speed!

"Perhaps it is not too late." Mudly swallowed a last worm. "I'll come along."

As they approached the marshy grass, they heard a long-drawn-out *wak*. It sounded like a cry.

"Something terrible must have happened," Bartleby whispered.

Mudly hmmphed. "It seems to me that ducks are always worrying." But he followed Bartleby toward the wakking anyway.

Mother Wak was flopped across her nest in a most undignified way. Her feathers were ruffled, and her eyes were frightened black slits.

"What is wrong?" Bartleby cried.

"Five-*wak*!" the duck muttered, as if she were talking to herself. "Only five! Little Six-*wak* is gone!"

"Little Six is gone!" Bartleby repeated. "Oh, it's my fault! If only I'd come back right after I escaped that raccoon."

"No, no, little Bartleby-*wak*! Don't blame yourself. I am sure you did what you could-*wak*!"

Bartleby's head drooped. "I hid instead of being brave. I didn't try to fight."

Zip hopped out of the nest and landed on Bartleby's carapace. Her little feet patted him comfortingly.

>*"When the Paw wants its dinner*
>*you can't be a winner.*
>*It does what it pleases*
>*and eats what it seizes.*
>*You had to hide*
>*or else you'd have died!"*

"Zip is right," Mudly agreed. "You can't be blamed for saving your own life. Besides, even if you'd come back, there was nothing you could have done."

Nothing you could have done. The words jabbed at Bartleby. What good was being from the Mighty Mississippi when he had no might himself?

"Will it be much longer until your eggs hatch?" Mudly asked Mother Wak.

The duck raised her head a bit. *"Wak!* Too long for safety."

Mudly emitted a little whiff of scent. "Minerva and I were going to have hatchlings one day. If you'd like, I could drip a circle of scent around your nest to discourage the Claw, the Paw, and the Jaw."

"Anything-*wak*! Anything to save my five egglets."

"I'm sure Mudly's odor would be a great help," Bartleby said. He wondered if Mother Wak's ducklings would smell like baby stinkpots when they hatched.

Zip hopped onto Mudly's shell. The stinkpot's eyes widened in surprise, but he didn't complain.

> *"Peepers start out as eggs,*
> *but I much prefer legs!*
> *Won't it be fun*
> *when Wak's egglets are done?"*

"Perhaps it will be pleasant. It's been a while since we've had ducklings in our water," Mudly replied. "For now, it is time for basking." He stretched his neck toward Bartleby. "Come along. The more you bask, the more you eat. The more you eat, the more you grow." He snapped up a moth that was hovering over a fluffy yellow flower. "And the bigger you are, the better you can defend yourself—and perhaps help your friends."

Bartleby followed Mudly toward the big water. But he couldn't help thinking that growing took much too long.

Junket

18

Bartleby and Mudly were basking on the great gray stone when a shiny black bird flew overhead. It dipped down so low, its wings stirred the water. "Caw?" it called. "Caw caw? Cawawaw!" Flapping noisily, it rose and circled the big water again.

"That bird is hunting for something," Bartleby said. "Do you think we should hide?"

Mudly stretched his neck and scanned the sky. "It's only Junket, searching for an easy meal. Don't worry—turtle shells are too much trouble for him."

But Bartleby kept his eyes on the noisy creature anyway. Once more, the bird began circling, then swooped down toward the basking rock. Bartleby drew his head in.

"Seen anything to eat?" the bird asked as it landed. It had the rough, scratchy voice of one who'd talked too much.

"There are tender leaves in the shallows," Bartleby

suggested, without poking his head out. "And fish fry if you're quick enough."

"Junket usually prefers something dead," Mudly said. "A furred creature like a squirrel, a mouse, or a shrew."

The black bird plucked at a mite underneath its wing. "Mmm, dead—even better if it's rotten. A spot of rot does wonders for the digestion."

"Sometimes a minnow washes up onshore," Bartleby said, edging his head out.

"Minnow would be good." Junket pulled at a feather on his back to smooth it. "Should eat lightly anyway. Been gorging on pizza and french fries lately."

Bartleby knew what pizza was. His boys used to eat it in front of the TV. It was drippy, red, and yellow. Long strands of it stuck to their chins. Bartleby wasn't sure whether he'd rather eat dead squirrel or pizza. They both looked disgusting. "Where did you eat pizza?" he asked. "Do you have boys?"

"Boys, no." Junket pecked at a sparkle on the basking stone. "Found new water place where humans go. Sharp edges all around, no mud at all. Water blue as Kingfisher over there. Tried to drink the stuff—ugh, bad! Got to drink soda instead."

"I've never heard of soda," Mudly said.

"Sweet, wet, fuzzy. Gets spilled everywhere. Garbage cans best of all. Filled with pizza and french fries."

Bartleby thought about this other water place. "Do you travel far?" he asked.

The bird puffed out his smooth, black chest. "All over. Seen everything. Been everywhere."

"Have you seen the Mighty Mississippi?"

Junket cocked his head. "Mis-sis-sippy? Of course! Sipped it up!"

Bartleby blinked. "You drank the Mississippi? But it's very, very big."

Junket pecked at a glittery spot on the basking stone. "Er, just a sip. Told you soda's too sweet."

"But the Mississippi's not a soda—it's a river!" Bartleby exclaimed. "Traveling water that's long and fast-flowing."

Junket scratched his back with a long, black toenail. "River? Seen fast water. Never heard of Mighty Mississippi."

"No?" Bartleby pulled his head in a little.

"Perhaps you could look for it the next time you travel," Mudly suggested.

"Find me a dead thing or two."

"Why don't you just hunt?" Bartleby asked.

"Too much bother. Dead food and garbage everywhere. And unguarded nests of eggs. Eggs never make trouble."

"Oh, there aren't any eggs around here," Bartleby said quickly. "But this morning in the woods across the water, I passed a dead mouse."

"Mouse? Mouse meat pretty good." Junket spread

his wings and flapped them. "I'll go take a look. Thanks for tip."

"It seems as if everyone around here likes eggs," Bartleby said glumly as the bird flew off.

"That was clever to send him in the other direction." Mudly snapped his jaws. "All that talk about food has made me rather hungry. Let's hunt!"

Bartleby was chasing a cluster of silvery fish fry through the lily pads when he heard sounds coming from the woods. Something big was approaching. He could hear it cracking twigs and crunching leaves. Its feet were sending dust into the air.

"Bartleby! Bartleby!"

"That sounds like a boy—my boy!" he whispered to Mudly. The two turtles hid among the lily pads and waited.

"Bartleby! Bartleby!" Davy emerged from the woods at the edge of the pond. Behind him came the twins. Bartleby couldn't help noticing that they were still pushing and shoving each other.

"I told you he wouldn't come when you called him, Davy. Bartleby's a turtle, not a dog," Jeff said.

"Yes, he will! He knows my voice. Hey, Bart! I got sick after I left you here. Mom made me stay in bed. But I knew you'd be okay 'cause you can hunt and dive. Come on, boy, let's go home!"

Bartleby's insides grew pleasantly warm, as if he'd been basking.

"Hey, Bart! Mom said if I found you we could get a real tank instead of your old bowl. Then you can really swim."

Bartleby's webs tingled, but he stayed hidden. He wasn't sure what a tank was, but he liked swimming.

"Look, I brought you some lettuce. Come on, boy!"

Bartleby felt a sharp, tangy sensation on his tongue. He poked his head up for a better look.

"Careful," Mudly whispered.

"Hey, Davy, over there! Ripples! Is that him? Come on, Bart. You must be tired of this mud hole. We'll bring you home where it's nice and safe. You can eat your yummy turtle flakes and watch all this wildlife stuff on TV."

Bartleby ducked under the water.

"Aw, shoot! Whatever was out there just disappeared. Anyway, I don't think that was your turtle, Davy. Come on."

"Yeah, let's get out of here. I told you we wouldn't find him. Ouch! There are too many mosquitoes in these woods—I bet I got a hundred bites already."

"Too many mosquitoes!" Mudly hmmphed. "If they're so smart, why don't they catch some?"

"No! We have to keep looking! We have to!"

Bartleby wondered if Davy was going to make rain with his eyes. Instead, he heard Jeff say, "Come on, Davy.

Maybe Mom will let you get a better pet. Wouldn't you rather have a puppy?"

Davy's friend, Amy, had a puppy, Bartleby remembered. She'd brought it to visit once. It was a noisy, drooling creature that tried to chew everything—including Bartleby. How could Jeff think it was a better pet?

"A puppy? Really? You think Mom would let me have one?"

"Sure. I bet the three of us can talk her into it."

Bartleby lifted his head in time to see the boys disappearing into the woods. The lettuce leaf was still on the mud bank where Davy had left it. He felt relieved, but a little sad, too. Boys weren't so bad. At least, not his boys.

He took a last look at the lettuce. "Come on," he said to Mudly. "Let's go find those fish fry."

Ssslip!

19

"Slip and Slide! Slide and Slip!
Now it's time to take a dip!"

Bartleby was bouncing wildly on a leaf as Zip, Webster, and Hopalot paddled around, trying to tip him. His raft wasn't a lily-pad leaf any longer, but a smaller, more slender one that they'd chewed off a flowering water plant.

"You're getting too good at lily pads," Webster had complained after Bartleby won six games in a row. "It's time you had more of a challenge."

"Must be where he's from," the kingfisher called from his branch above the water. "River turtles are probably used to rocking and rolling with the flow."

In a way they were right, Bartleby thought. Playing Slip! had become less challenging. What's more, the game wasn't the only thing that was easier. Each day it seemed as if the flies were flying a little slower. And that the basking stone was moving a bit closer to shore.

His naps were changing, too. Whenever he closed his eyes, he felt a pull that was irresistible. A flow that swept him away on a wild and thrilling ride.

Bartleby was trying to recall the feeling of the rushing water when Hopalot suddenly whizzed over his shell. Surprised, the red-ear jerked his head sideways—and upset the leaf. To the cheers of his opponents, he splashed into the water.

"Got you that time!" Webster exclaimed.

"You did, all right!" Bartleby said as he popped up at the surface. "Let's play again tomorrow." He didn't much mind that the game was over. He wanted to take a nap so he could return to the flowing water. He hoped he was right about where it was taking him.

"Pleasant eating!" Webster called as he paddled away.

Bartleby was almost to the basking stone when he noticed a long shadow. It seemed to be drifting straight toward him. He narrowed his gaze and saw two nostrils . . . two eye bumps . . . and the pointy tip of a tail.

"Sssalutations!" the alligator called.

Bartleby looked around, but there was nowhere to hide.

"I was just chasing minnows across the water." Seezer flicked his tail. "Ssslow, ssstupid things. No challenge at all."

"This morning I found some delicious fry among

the lilies," Bartleby said, back-paddling a few strokes. "Maybe you should swim over there."

Seezer sniffed. "Fry—hardly worth the effort. I miss the fish in my beautiful bayou. The paddlefish with its duckish sssnout! The sssavage gar! How I long for battle! I wish you could sssee them."

"I'd like that," Bartleby murmured, but he wondered if the paddlefish and the gar ate red-eared turtles.

Seezer looked down his snout at Bartleby. "Would you?"

Bartleby tucked his head in a bit. "Someday—when I'm bigger. I'm not sure I could swim in such fast water yet."

Seezer flicked his tail again. "Ssso, you've ssseen the Mississippi in your dreams! Do you know the way home now?"

Bartleby trembled.

Seezer prodded him with his snout. "Tell me."

Bartleby closed his eyes. "I dreamed of drifting in traveling water. At first, it wasn't very fast or wide. But as it flowed, it changed. It met other waters on its journey. They joined and spread. They surged and roared. At last, they became one great water path. . . . I believe it may have been the Mighty Mississippi."

"Home!" Seezer's eyes glinted. He smacked his tail and set the surface of the water rocking. "I will leave tonight. Tell me where the journey sssstarts."

Bartleby bobbed up and down.

The jaws jabbed at Bartleby once more. "Well?"

"That is the part I don't know yet. But I am sure I will find out soon."

Seezer's black eyes flashed. "I've already told you alligators have little patience. Ssstill, I sssuppose I can wait a ssshort while longer. As sssoon as you know the ssstarting place, you must come to my cave. It's there across the water, just under the mud bank." The alligator sank down. "Yes, Bartleby, you must come and sssee. It's very tight and cozy inssside. And I will greet you with a warm welcome. *Mississippi-ssstyle.*"

"Hmmph! It sounds like that alligator wants a homestyle snack before he leaves." Mudly was plodding around the outside of Mother Wak's nest. Yellow drops leaked from under the edge of his shell, leaving a putrid trail. "Once you tell him where to start the trip," Mudly said, "he won't need you anymore—except maybe as a meal."

Mudly's odor was so strong, Bartleby couldn't help pulling his head in. He was sure no Claw or Paw or Jaw would approach the nest now. Mother Wak's egglets would be safe, through they would be seriously smelly. "Maybe Seezer will be so grateful to know the way, he'll leave me alone," he replied, trying to open his mouth as little as possible.

"Seezer is a growing alligator. With each passing day, his appetite increases. Who can say if he will crave turtle for supper one night?" Mudly disappeared around the side of the nest. "The sooner he leaves, the safer we'll be."

> *"Yes! Peepers too will cheer the day*
> *when the 'gator goes away."*

Zip leapt off the edge of the nest. She hopped up and down as if Seezer were already gone.

There was a great flurry of flapping as Mother Wak burst through the mud grass. "Egglets-*wak*! I'm back-*wak*!" She waddled up to the nest to examine the eggs—and thrust her bill under her wing. "*Wak-wak!* Disgusting-*wak*! Exactly like rotten eggs!" she cried. "Thank you, turtle-*wak*!" With her bill still under her wing, she mounted the nest.

Mudly pulled his head in. He wasn't used to so much praise.

Bartleby watched Mother Wak settle gently down on her eggs. He felt a funny softness under his plastron. If he lived in the Mighty Mississippi, he could meet a female red-ear. There might even be red-ear eggs.

"Mother Wak, have you ever flown over any traveling water around here?" he asked.

"*Wak!* Traveling water-*wak*?" The duck pulled her bill out from under her wing for a moment. "I don't think so, Bartleby-*wak*. Why do you ask?"

"I think it may be the way to the Mighty Mississippi. At least I hope so. If I find it soon, I can send the alligator far from here." Bartleby's webs trembled. "And if I don't, I think he will eat me."

Mother Wak stretched her neck over her nest and

nudged Bartleby gently. "After the egglets are hatched, Bartleby-*wak*, I will fly about and find some traveling water for you. It won't be too much longer-*wak*! I have already heard tapping from inside the egglets-*wak*!"

"You will-*wak*! I mean, you will?" Bartleby said. "Thank you!" Above his plastron he felt a tapping, too.

Suddenly, he was very tired. He felt the need to restore himself with a turtle nap, to dream about the Mighty Mississippi.

"When the air is mild and muggy,
and the lily patch gets buggy,
we feast on 'squito, fly, and gnat
and stuff our bellies till they're fat."

In the warm, humid evening, Zip peeped her song over and over. The lily-pad patch was filled with creatures eating, playing, and singing. They held contests to see who could snap up the most mosquitoes. The frogs gave concerts. The turtles had shell-bumping matches, trying to tip each other over backward.

Mudly was the first to leave. "Too much noise. Too crowded," he grumbled. "Good night, Bartleby."

"Good night! I'll see you at sunrise."

In a little while, Webster and the other paints left for their boggy log. Zip and Hopalot settled under a clump of slimy leaves. The spotted salamander slipped into the marsh grass. Bully and the other bigfrogs were the last to depart. Each wanted to be the one to sing the final song of the evening.

Bartleby was tired, but he didn't want to find shelter. He wanted to sleep out in the exquisitely sticky air all night. He chose a gently rocking lily pad and settled down. The floaty feeling started almost instantly.

He felt a bump beneath his plastron. This turtle nap is going to be exciting! he thought. He squeezed his eyes shut tighter and waited. He saw the whirl of colors. He felt a breeze tickle his carapace. He heard its long, whispering hiss.

Breeze? The sticky evening had been perfectly still. Bartleby opened his eyes.

"That looked like a lovely gathering, friend," a voice said. "I wish I could have been a part of it."

Bartleby squinted. In a patch of water lit by moonlight he could see a long, curving shadow. His heart began to flutter like a giant moth. He knew who that voice belonged to—and it was no friend of his.

"Sadly, I am always left out of social gatherings. Can you tell me why, friend?"

Bartleby knew why, but he kept quiet.

"Is this the silent treatment?" the snake hissed. "Oh, how disappointing! I thought you might be different from the others. I thought you might truly try to be my friend." The snake opened its mouth and flicked its tongue. Then it began weaving toward Bartleby's lily pad.

"Stay where you are, and I will be glad to talk to you!" Bartleby burst out.

"Talk? Excellent, friend! I will just come a little closer so we don't have to shout."

"No, stop! I can hear you perfectly."

"All right, friend, let us talk. We'll get to know each other." The snake stopped flowing and floated on the surface. "Tell me, do you like caves?"

Bartleby tried to keep his voice from quavering. "Caves?"

"You know, friend. Dark, cozy places, the way I imagine it is inside your shell."

"They're nice," Bartleby replied.

"Would you like to see my cave, friend?"

Bartleby blinked. "You have a cave?"

"Yes, I carry it with me, just as you carry yours with you. Take a look, friend." The snake opened its mouth.

Bartleby stared into the whitish pink space. Two long, pointy teeth glistened in the moonlight. "It's dark and narrow at the back," he murmured.

"Dark, yes. Difficult to see. Why don't you come closer, friend?"

Bartleby scrambled backward on the lily pad. "I've seen enough!" he cried.

"If you are truly my friend, you must accept my invitation."

"Friends invite—they don't insist," Bartleby said. "If

you force me, I cannot be your friend." Suddenly, he felt something behind him. The snake's tail was stroking his carapace!

"Pardon me, friend. I didn't mean to be pushy. Please accept my hospitality." The wriggly tongue tickled Bartleby's plastron.

"Your cave is nothing but a mouth! If I enter, you will eat me—and friends don't eat each other!" Bartleby exclaimed.

"But that's not true! I have eaten many fine friends. I couldn't help myself. The desire to be close just overwhelms me." The snake opened its jaws. "So good-bye, old friend. I will miss you."

With all the willpower he could muster, Bartleby fought to keep himself from withdrawing into his shell. Instead he stretched out his legs and made them as stiff as wood. He hooked his sharp, tiny nails around the outside of the snake's mouth.

The snake unhinged its lower jaw and made its mouth even wider. It tried to swallow. Half of Bartleby was inside the creature's mouth, and half of him was out. But he was still holding fast to the snake's jaw. It rolled its head back and forth, trying to loosen Bartleby's grip. But the red-ear only dug his nails farther into the snake's tight skin.

The furious snake clamped its powerful jaws down on Bartleby's carapace. They pressed harder and harder until Bartleby began to feel he would be crushed.

Then he heard a deep booming *rrroak*! The water seemed to explode with splashing. Bully!

"My tail! Stop biting my tail!" the snake cried. "Oh, oh, let go!" For a moment its jaws loosened. Just as quickly, it bit down again.

Above the water, Bartleby sensed something stirring. He heard wings beating and a dry, rough cry. Still trapped in the snake's jaws, he felt himself lifted up and out of the water. Higher and higher into the night sky.

And then—*splash!* He hit the water's surface and was free. Stunned, he paddled to the mud bank and looked up.

The kingfisher flew to its branch with the snake gripped in its beak. Though the snake writhed and whipped its tail, the kingfisher kept its hold, slapping the creature against the tree over and over. Finally, Bartleby saw a long, limp body fall into the grass.

"*Ak ak ak!*" The kingfisher gave a sharp, triumphant cry and flew off into the woods.

The Trade

22

In the morning, Bartleby swam to the basking stone to tell Mudly what had happened.

"Hmmph! I suppose Bully will be boasting about his battle for a long time to come," Mudly said. "But I am very glad he helped the kingfisher to save you."

Bartleby stretched his neck toward the bright sun. "I won't mind Bully's bragging. He was awfully brave to distract the snake so the kingfisher could attack."

"Kingfisher is a fine hunter," Mudly said. "And I know he doesn't like snakes. They are nest raiders and egg eaters."

Bartleby turned his head toward Mudly. "Egg eaters? Do you mean they steal the eggs of birds that nest in trees?"

"Yes. Snakes are good climbers."

"And do they also like the eggs of nests in the grass?"

Mudly emitted a foul smell. He turned to Bartleby. "Perhaps they do."

A cawing above them made the turtles look up. A shiny black bird was circling the big water place.

"Anything to eat around here?" Junket called as he flapped down on the stone.

"There is lots of food for those who aren't lazy," Mudly replied.

But Bartleby had an idea. "I believe I know where you can find a dead snake."

"Snake—where?"

Bartleby took his time answering. "Let me think." He snapped at a passing moth. "Did you find the river? The Mighty Mississippi?"

Junket scratched under a wing. "Not exactly. Not flying much. Been staying at the place of the bright blue water. Too much pizza. Snake sounds good."

"It was a long, fat snake, too," Bartleby said. "But first tell me. Did you see traveling water?"

Junket pecked at a long, skinny toe. "Saw some. Not far from here."

Bartleby felt a sharp pull in his middle. "A river?"

"Nope. Not a river."

"What do you mean? Is it fast?"

"Nope. Not fast."

"Is it deep?"

"Nope. Not deep."

"Is it going somewhere?"

"Yep. Definitely going somewhere."

"Then tell me how to get there!"

Junket eyed Bartleby sharply. "Be easier if you could fly." He flapped his wings. "On foot, you go through the woods. Past the humans' houses. Across the school yard where kids drop lunch crusts. Beyond the field of holes with eggs that don't crack. Over the great road where fast cars leave carcasses of creatures."

Over a great road. A shiver of fear ran through Bartleby.

"Where's my snake?"

"In the grass below the kingfisher's branch."

Junket flapped his wings. "Travel at night," he advised as he began to rise. "That's what bats say. Wait till then, might have a chance."

Might! Bartleby thought.

"Time for breakfast. 'Bye!" Junket flew off.

"Pleasant eating," Mudly called. He turned to Bartleby. "That snake took many from our community. Now it is giving something back. You will be able to send Seezer on his way. We'll all be free of him."

"Yes," Bartleby agreed. But he felt the pull in his middle again. It was a bit like being hungry, only he didn't want food. He wanted to see the flowing water, too. Eagerly, he stretched his neck toward the sun, closed his eyes, and waited.

Dark Journey

23

The evening was warm and breezy. Bartleby rested on the mud bank and watched the sky. Sometimes rippled, sometimes smooth, it reminded him of a big water place. He imagined it was the Mighty Mississippi and that he was swimming in it.

When he got drowsy, he slipped into the water. The mud, which was especially warm under the shallows, had become his favorite place to spend the night. He had just begun tucking himself under it when something stirred the water just above him. Quickly, Bartleby pulled his head in.

Lap-lop-plip-plop! Something was lapping the water with a long, curled tongue. "Mama, I'm hungry!" a voice yipped.

"Hunger is good! An appetite makes an able hunter even better." *Sniff, sniff, sniff!* "There's something delicious on the breeze tonight. I sense it hiding under the foul stench of Stinkpot."

"Whoever that creature is, it has a clever nose," Bartleby said to himself. As quietly as he could, he edged his head out and looked up through the water. In the wavery moonlight he saw a shimmer of silvery fur, the steady glow of two yellow eyes, and teeth as fine and sharp as pine needles.

"Ooh, what is that scent, Mama?" another little voice yipped.

Sniff, sniff, sniff. "It's a duck dinner. That means rich, juicy meat."

"Yip-yippi-yay!"

"Yippi-yippi-yee!"

"Yip-yip-yip-yip!"

"Yip-yippi-yip!"

"Hush! Be silent or your meal will fly away." *Sniff, sniff, sniff!* "I smell more. Eggs for dessert!"

"What's an egg, Mama?"

"The most perfect food in the woods. Outside, it looks like a smooth, round rock. But inside, there's a surprise. A soft, gooey treat—or a tiny, tender birdlet. Now let me see . . ." *Sniff, sniff, sniff!* "I smell five eggs. One for each of us. Finish your drink and get ready for a long hunt. Ducks are clever at hiding their nests."

Bartleby didn't dare move from the shallows until they were gone. He was afraid the mother beast might sniff him with her sharp nose. Or see him with her sharp eyes. Or bite him with her sharp teeth. But he had to help Mother Wak!

He remembered Zip's words after little Six had been stolen:

When the Paw wants its dinner
you can't be a winner.

But instead of making him want to give up, the words made Bartleby want to resist. Maybe he wasn't big or fast. But he was hard. Stubborn and steady. Dependable and determined.

He pushed away from the mud and headed downward. The water above him became deeper and deeper. After he'd escaped from the raccoon, he'd never been down to the bottom of the big water again. And now it was night. There wasn't even the dimmest light to help him see. He had to feel his way. In and out of the water grass. Past coils of twisted roots and fuzzy rocks. Over mounds of rotting leaves and the pulsing shapes of bottom creatures.

At first he wasn't sure where he was going. All he knew was that he couldn't let the Claw, the Jaw, or the Paw rob the nest again.

After a while, he reached a great dark shape rising firmly from the muddy bottom. Carefully, Bartleby touched it with a forefoot. It was harder than a turtle shell. Rough and familiar. Bartleby swam alongside it for a while.

"This must be the bottom of the basking stone," he

said to himself. "I am in the middle of the big water." But his webs were still tingling and pulsing. They were taking Bartleby even farther away.

His eyes were becoming accustomed to the dimness now. He tried to stay clear of the clusters of fish that hung at the bottom. Their stillness made them seem asleep, but their lidless eyes stared eerily. Their mouths pulsed open and closed as if testing for prey.

An underwater plant swayed as he passed. It was silly to be afraid of a plant, he knew. Just in case, he stayed away from its straying tendrils. But a great black beetle lunged at him from behind a stalk. It had a bulgy black eye on either side of its head, and a frightening, hairy belly. Bartleby froze. Should he swim away or hide in his shell? Before he could decide, the thing snatched at him with its two big pincers and grabbed him by the front edge of his carapace.

With his webs, Bartleby tried to push the great beetle away. But it pulled him forward, toward its wide-open jaws. Bartleby jerked into his shell to keep from having his head snapped off. *Aaack!* The beetle bit the edge of his carapace. It opened its jaws and rasped, "RrrOCK!" Bartleby felt himself being jiggled with a violent, heaving motion, as if the beetle were trying to shake him out of his shell. He tucked himself in tighter and waited.

At last, the pincers released him. He peeked out. The beetle was swimming off, its antennae trembling crazily.

Exhausted, Bartleby drifted down and settled on the bottom.

The feel of the slime cradling his plastron made him want to dig deeper and hide. He loved the way it tugged at his claws. He loved its silkiness between his webs. He couldn't resist nudging his snout into it. A dreamy calm began to overtake him.

He let his eyes close. But instead of a rushing river, he saw a silver-furred beast with yellow eyes. That creature and her family are hunting for Mother Wak and the eggs! Bartleby suddenly remembered. He snapped his head above the slime. He waggled his tail and twisted his neck this way and that. He blew out a stream of bubbles like a silent roar and began paddling away as fast as he could.

He'd never been to the place he was heading now. He'd never seen what he was looking for. Yet he had an idea in his mind. A deep, dark place. A cold, damp hole. He tried to guess what would be inside. Mud and leaves? Jellylike eggs? Slimy slugs? The remains of creatures who had strayed inside?

Moonlight began filtering through the dark water. It's shallower here, Bartleby thought. The mud bank can't be much farther. He paddled faster, pushing against roots and plants. His rear webs flicked away bits of mud and leaves. Once they brushed a flat-headed bottom fish that wriggled and writhed at being touched. Terrified, Bartleby swerved away.

Finally, through a forest of water grass, he thought he saw a mud wall. He swam along the length and soon found a hole. A slurping noise came from deep inside. His heart began to beat faster. "It is only the sound of water flowing in and out of empty space," he said, trying to calm himself.

Empty space. All at once he knew! It was the thing that he'd been searching for all along. Only this place was more than a hole. It was a cave.

Trapped!

24

Bartleby paddled quietly up to the big, dark hole. "Seezer?" he called. There was no answer. He called louder. "Seezer! Are you in there?"

"Why, I believe I sssmell the red-ear. What a sssurprise! Come in, Bartleby."

Bartleby treaded water outside the black hole. "I can't— I'm in a great hurry. But I must talk to you. It's urgent!"

"*I sssaid, come in!*" Seezer's long, powerful tail whipped out of the hole and swept Bartleby inside.

Bartleby could feel a thick layer of mud and mucky leaves under his webs. The smell of rot was overwhelming. It was too dark for him to see anything except Seezer's glowing red eyes. Then he felt the alligator's snout poke him.

"Have you come to tell me where to begin the journey back to my bayou?" The red eyes flashed.

"No. I came to ask you to help me save a friend and her family," Bartleby blurted out.

"What sssort of friend?"

Bartleby hesitated. He knew Seezer was not going to like his answer. "A web-footed friend," he said in a small voice. "A mother duck."

"Sssave a web-footed creature?" Seezer roared. "You insssult me! A great beast sssuch as I does not sssave ducks. He ssswallows them!"

"But Mother Wak is no ordinary duck," Bartleby protested. "She let me sleep in her nest to keep me safe. She even offered to help search for traveling water—the place to begin your quest."

"Web-footed birds are my sssworn enemies. You will have to find traveling water sssome other way!"

"Perhaps I already know where to find it," Bartleby said, backpaddling out of the dark hole, "if that crow was right."

The great jaws snapped. "What? You have the directions? Tell me!"

"They're long and complicated, and I've no time to lose," Bartleby said, slipping out into the open water. "I must return to the nest and try to help my friend. You will have to wait." As fast as he could, he began swimming away.

"Ssstop!" Seezer bellowed.

But Bartleby only paddled harder, back toward the other side of the big water.

Even before he reached the shore, Bartleby could hear a shrill song carrying over the water:

"Creatures, awake! Creatures, arise!
Here is the Jaw with the bright yellow eyes.
She's hunting for egglets, so please heed our plight.
If we all band together, we'll rout her tonight!

"Creatures, be brave! Creatures, please hurry.
Make the fox-wak and her four fox-kits scurry!"

"Fox-*waks*!" Bartleby repeated, shuddering as he slid out of the water and climbed up the mud bank. He felt very small and helpless. He had no plan. But he plodded on as quickly as he could.

From behind a curtain of grass, he peered at the nest. Mother Wak was atop it, but Bartleby barely recognized her. Her chest was puffed out and her wings were spread. She snapped her bill as fiercely as any Claw, Paw, or Jaw.

The mother fox and her kits were circling Mother Wak in a low, sneaky gait. Every few steps the mother fox darted forward, snarling and nipping. At each snap, Mother Wak beat her wings so hard she nearly flew off the nest.

Bartleby stood quietly for a moment. Then he rushed into the circle of foxes.

"I order you to leave at once!" he commanded.

The fox kits ran behind their mother. "What's that?" one of them asked.

"*Sniff, sniff, sniff!* It's just a turtle. Barely big enough to bother with. Pay no attention to it."

"I said, stop!" Bartleby shouted again. He tromped on the mother fox's paw. "Go find your dinner elsewhere."

Her yellow eyes glared at him. "What a senseless creature. Too stupid even to crawl away. What do you care about duck eggs?"

"I am Bartleby of the Mighty Mississippi. And Mother Wak is my friend. I warn you, you are in danger if you continue attacking."

The mother fox's laugh rang out, high and mocking. She lowered her head until her black nose was touching Bartleby's carapace. Then she gave him a lick with her pink curled tongue.

Quickly, Bartleby thrust his head up and bit her nose! He clamped down firmly on the cold, clammy knob.

"*Aaaoooooo!*" the fox yelped. Crying, her kits ran into the grass to hide.

Bartleby was snapped back and forth as the fox shook her head and pawed at her nose. He struggled to hold on, and then suddenly he was tossed into the air.

Smack! He came down hard in the dirt. A black-nailed paw reached out for him. It rolled him over onto his back. In a panic, he paddled the air.

"Children, you can come out now," the fox called. "Here's a plaything for you."

A sharp little paw swatted at Bartleby. "Yip-yippi-yay! Look, it can spin!"

"Yippi-yippi-yee! Let me try!" Another paw batted him the other way.

"Yip-yip-yip-yip! It's my turn!" A paw dragged him across the ground.

"Yip-yippi-yip! Give it to me!" Sharp little nails scratched at his plastron.

Inside his shell, Bartleby tucked up even tighter. He had to struggle to breathe. He almost wished the kits would eat him and get it over with. But they didn't seem interested. He wondered if he could be spun to death.

He felt a springy vibration underneath him. He tried to make his muddled head focus. Something was coming toward them. It seemed to be hopping. No, it was crawling. Flying. Running!

All at once, the kits stopped yipping. The fox stopped snarling. Even Mother Wak stopped squawking. Still on his back, Bartleby poked his head out in time to see Bully spring into the clearing. Zip and Hopalot were close behind him. A moment later, Mudly and Webster appeared. There was a flapping above. The kingfisher settled in a tree and gave a short, sharp cry.

The mother fox's jeering laughter broke the silence. "What's this? More dinner guests? Good! We'll have a feast!"

"If you don't leave now, you and your kits may be the dinner," the kingfisher said.

"Ha! Who's going to eat me? You? Those frogs? The turtles? I could eat any of you in one bite, but you're barely worth the trouble."

She was answered by a series of bellows that shook even the trees.

"*Whaaat's thaaat?*" The fox kits wailed.

In another moment, Seezer came bounding through the grass, using his tail as a catapult. "Did sssomeone sssay dinner? Am I invited, too?"

The mother fox backed up a few steps. "Do you like duck?"

"I detest duck."

The fox pricked up her ears. "Then perhaps you like to eat greens. We have quite a selection of frogs and turtles." She batted Bartleby with her paw. "Here, you can start with this one. He's been making a nuisance of himself. Why, he actually had the nerve to bite me."

Seezer pounded his tail on the ground. "Turn him over at once!"

Bartleby felt himself flipped right side up. He took a deep breath, and his head began to clear.

"What do you want?" the mother fox whispered.

"I want you to go away."

The fox emitted her high laugh. "Oh, but that's silly when there is such a bountiful dinner before us."

"Go before I decide to have *fox* for dinner!" Seezer roared.

The mother fox stepped backward lightly. "Those eggs are smelly anyway. They're probably rotten."

"Perhaps you are right. But your kits will be fresh and tender." Seezer snapped his jaws.

"Run! Run away, kits! Now!" The fox and her family fled for the woods.

Bartleby poked his head out of his shell. He hoped Seezer wasn't planning to eat Mother Wak himself—or red-eared turtle. "Wh . . . what are you doing here?" he stammered.

In the moonlight, Seezer's eyes flashed angrily. "Your foolish behavior forced me to come. I had to make sssure my directions weren't devoured by those foxes. Have you forgotten? You haven't yet told me where the traveling water is!"

"Oh . . . the directions." Bartleby let out a long breath. He closed his eyes and tried to remember the journey

129

Junket had described. "It's through the woods, past the humans' houses—"

"Not now," Seezer interrupted. "You must tell me in the daylight. In the morning it will be easier for me to remember."

Bartleby was perplexed. Had Seezer come for the directions or not? "But you said alligators are impatient. Are you certain you don't want to get on your way tonight?"

Sharp as a bolt of lightning, Seezer's tail cracked the ground. "You're not trying to get rid of me, are you, Bartleby?"

"No, of course not," Bartleby answered quickly.

"Good, because being from the Mighty Mississippi, we are almost relatives. Kissing cousins. You wouldn't want to get rid of your kissing cousin?" Seezer poked Bartleby with his snout. "Ah, your sssmell makes my mouth water for bayou edibles. I will return to my den now to prepare myself for the journey." Slowly, he began crawling toward the big water. "Perhaps when you are rested, you will want to sssee it your-ssself."

Bartleby blinked. "See it?"

"We will ssspeak tomorrow," Seezer replied, heading into the marsh grass.

Above his battered plastron, Bartleby felt a stirring. He wasn't certain if it was excitement or fear. "Do you mean go with you to the place where the traveling water starts?" he called.

"Sssuit yourself," Seezer said, looking back.

Bartleby felt a current so strong, it made his blood rush. For an instant, he heard the dull roar of surging water. "I would like to see the real thing—even if it's just the very beginning," he said dreamily.

"The beginning!" Seezer practically snorted the words. "No, I don't sssuppose you would dare to go farther. Perhaps the Mighty Mississippi isn't your true home, after all. If it was, you would do anything to return there."

"It is and I would!" Bartleby retorted.

"Then you are planning to go?"

Bartleby's heart was beating so hard, he imagined every creature in the pond could hear it. "Yes."

"A sssmall turtle like you? Why, you've never been anywhere. How will you know the ways of a river? Where to find food and where to rest? Who is friend and who is foe?"

"Maybe I could go with you," Bartleby whispered, terrified of his own words.

"You? Why would I want to take you with me?"

"I might prove useful. And two travelers might have more luck than one."

"Useful? A creature who sssleeps under a duck's bottom? Ha!" The grass began to sway as Seezer walked off.

The alligator's words wounded Bartleby as sharply as a fox's tooth. Perhaps Seezer was right, he thought. He wasn't brave enough to call the Mississippi his home. Miserably, he pulled his head in.

But he couldn't shut out Seezer's voice. Like the breeze, it slipped under his shell and inside his head. "All right, Bartleby. I'll conssssider your request. For now, return to the sssafety of the duck's nest. A night ssspent under a mother's care ssshould help ressstore you."

Brother-wak!

26

Bartleby awoke cradled by dry grass and soft feathers. He was inside Mother Wak's nest, but something was different. Instead of the steady ticking of the egg's heartbeats, he heard tiny peeps all around him. Slowly he poked his head out.

"Welcome, Brother-*wak*!" a friendly voice piped. "We've been waiting for you-*wak*!"

Bartleby saw five small, dampish birds staring at him. Their bills were flat, and their feet were webbed just like their mother's. But instead of the soft, weathered brown of Mother Wak's feathers, theirs were yellow and fuzzy. Bartleby opened his mouth to greet them—and clamped it shut again. The babies were cute, but they were smelly.

"Last one out is a rotten egglet—that's you-*wak*!" the closest duckling teased. Bartleby couldn't believe the plump little thing had fit into a shell just last night.

"We're going swimming-*wak*!" another duckling informed him. "Mother's going to teach us!"

"We're going to eat, too! *Wak-wak-wak!*" a third duckling added.

"And fly someday-*wak!*" a fourth duckling exclaimed. "Better come out of that shell-*wak!*"

Mother Wak poked her head over the side of the nest. "Silly ducklets! Bartleby-*wak*'s a turtle. His shell is a part of him-*wak!*"

"But where are his wings? How will Bartleby-*wak* fly with us?" the fifth duckling asked.

"A turtle-*wak* doesn't need wings. He doesn't need to fly. Bartleby-*wak* can swim a long, long way. He can dive. He can breathe under the water."

"But what's inside his shell?" the plump duckling asked.

"Courage and conviction!" Mother Wak answered. "Now, enough questions! Everybody into the water. Come along. *Wak, wak, wak!*"

"Are you coming too, Bartleby-*wak*?" the littlest duckling asked.

"Maybe later," Bartleby replied. He plodded back through the grass and slipped into the water. A little farther up the mud bank, he saw the babies lined up behind their mother, bobbing and *wakking* with glee. Bartleby felt strangely sad. Instead of joining them, he dove under the surface and paddled out to the basking stone.

He could hardly believe that swimming to the center of the pond had once felt like an endless journey. Now it took no effort at all. He crawled up the side of the stone and found Mudly and Zip watching the ducklings, too.

"Those babies are making the biggest racket we've ever had in our water," the stinkpot grumbled. "It's nearly impossible to nap."

"They smell just like you," Bartleby told him.

Mudly took another look at the line of ducklings. "They do? Perhaps I will visit them later. It is strange how things work out sometimes."

Bartleby stretched his head toward the sun and closed his eyes. "The ducklings are lucky to have this big water place for a home."

"Yes, it's a good place to begin one's life," Mudly agreed.

Bartleby opened his eyes. "What do you mean? Won't the ducklings always live here?"

"Oh, no. When they are big enough, they will fly off to seek mates. Then they will find nesting places of their own."

Zip hopped up and down in agreement.

> "When pond creatures grow, they often go.
> I, too, will soon roam
> from my watery home."

"Do you mean you are moving to the other side of the big water, Zip?" Bartleby asked.

"I will live in the wood
as a grown peeper should.
It's how we evolve
once our tails dissolve.
It's time to make room
for new tadpoles to zoom!"

Bartleby glanced over to see her tail. To his amazement, it was completely gone. He couldn't imagine the big water without her. When he'd been a pet, it had seemed as if every day was the same. But here in the outside world, things—and creatures—were constantly changing.

"This big water place is the best home I have ever known," he told his friends. "Yet, I long to see the Mississippi and to meet other red-ears."

Mudly let out a small, sharp scent. "The need to find home is the way of many creatures. It is a very powerful thing. If you feel it, perhaps you must go."

"Seezer might let me accompany him to the Mighty Mississippi," Bartleby admitted.

"If you travel with that long-jawed beast,
you might turn out to be his feast!"

Zip's voice was as high and shrill as a cry of danger.

Miserably, Bartleby pulled his head in. "The way to the river is sure to be long and dangerous. Even if he didn't eat me, I might not survive it."

PART **Three**

Through the Woods

27

Bartleby rested on the mud bank, waiting for his friends and watching the sun go down. Over and over he repeated Junket's directions until they became a little chant. *Through the woods. Past the humans' houses. Across the school yard. Beyond the field of holes. Over the great road.*

The sky darkened and a round moon rose. Gradually, he was surrounded by creatures—Mudly, Zip, Mother Wak, Bully, Kingfisher, Muskrat, Hopalot, and Webster. So many friends. And now he was leaving them. For Seezer had agreed to let Bartleby go with him to the Mighty Mississippi.

"There's plenty of light. Perfect for ssstarting our journey," Seezer observed. He flicked his tail back and forth, back and forth.

"Perfect for the Paw, the Claw, and the Jaw to hunt!" Mother Wak fluttered her wings. "Be careful, Bartleby-*wak*!"

"I'll sing about you, Bartleby,
I'll say that you're so smartleby.
The Paw, the Claw, and Jaw could never
eat a red-ear that's so clever!"

"Thank you, Zip," Bartleby said. "You've been a good friend. I'll miss our games of Slip!" He turned to the rest of them. "I'll miss all of you. Bully, Kingfisher, Muskrat—you saved me from the snake. And Mother Wak, you protected me from the Paw, the Claw, and the Jaw. Thank you for being my friends."

He turned to Mudly and nudged the stinkpot's shell with his head. "If I hadn't met you when I first arrived here, I would have starved to death. Are you certain you don't want to come along with us?"

"No, this water place is enough for me." Mudly snapped up a passing moth and chewed it slowly. "Besides, last night I smelled the scent of a female *Sternotherus oderatus* on the breeze. Soon I will begin looking for her."

"Perhaps you'll have hatchlings," Bartleby said. In the darkness he imagined tiny stinkpots floating among the lily pads like new blossoms. He wished he could be there to see them.

"Perhaps," Mudly agreed. "And I'll be sure to tell them about the days when a red-eared turtle and an alligator lived in our water place. Good-bye, friend. Although we

140

Sternotherus oderatuses are solitary creatures, I will miss you." In an instant, he slipped into the water. "Pleasant eating," he called, and disappeared beneath the surface.

Bartleby led the way to the path through the woods. The last time he'd been there, he'd been carried in Davy's pocket. He'd only *heard* the woods. Now he looked around. The leafy treetops shut out most of the moonlight. Rustling sounds were everywhere, but he couldn't see what was making them. He felt as if he'd already been swallowed up by the strange surroundings. As if he were inside a giant living creature.

Behind him, he could hear Seezer's swishing walk. The alligator's breath came out in grunts. They were both more comfortable in water. On land they were awkward and clumsy. What if the traveling water was too far to reach by crawling?

Bartleby wasn't even sure he could crawl to the other end of the path. How could he expect to make it past houses, beyond a school yard, across a field, and over a road?

A terrible screech made him look up. A bird with round, glowing eyes and horny tufts swooped toward him, its great, curved claws open. Terrified, Bartleby ducked into his shell. In a moment he would be in the air. Flying!

The air above him *whooshed*, sending bits of leaf and

twig swirling. A wing tip brushed his shell. There was a screech—and a great flapping noise as the creature flew on.

Now Bartleby was certain he was making a terrible mistake. Even if he did get to the bayou, he would never survive there! The moment he entered the warm, sweet water, he would become dinner for a bird, or a snake, or a giant fish. But he kept his fears to himself and continued along the path.

Farther away from the pond, the dirt became dry and dusty. It seeped into Bartleby's throat and eyes and made him crawl even more slowly. He tried to think about fast-traveling water. To feel its energy in his webs. "I am going to the Mighty Mississippi," he told himself.

"I'm afraid you'll have to change your plans," a strange voice said.

Suddenly, Bartleby was facing an animal he'd never seen before. It hung by its long hairless tail from a low branch. It had a pale, furry body and a whiskered, rat-like snout with many teeth.

The creature reached out and grabbed Bartleby. Then it swung itself up into the tree.

Bartleby thought quickly. "Thank you for saving me," he said.

The creature held him up in front of its pale, twitching face. "Saving you? In a way, I suppose I am. I'm saving you for my dinner."

"Oh, I don't mind. I'd definitely prefer to be eaten by

you than by that creature down there. He was going to take me back to his cold, dark den under the water and let me rot. I'd much rather be eaten quickly."

Bartleby's captor looked down at Seezer and blinked its dark eyes. "What kind of creature is it, anyway?"

"It's a giant tree-leaping lizard," said Bartleby.

The paw gripped Bartleby more tightly. "I've never heard of one."

"Probably because anyone who's ever seen it has been eaten up. You've heard of tree frogs, haven't you?"

"Yes, but they're small and springy. That thing doesn't look like it can leap."

Seezer snapped his jaws. "If I leap up there, I will carry you both down to my underwater den."

"I hate water!" the creature squealed.

"Then give me back my turtle!" Seezer bellowed. He hunched his body, curled his tail, and catapulted himself at the tree.

The animal shrieked and hurled Bartleby toward the ground. Bartleby felt himself shoot downward. Good-bye, Seezer, good-bye, Mississippi, he thought.

Ploosh! Bartleby's plastron struck something soft and light. "Hey, get off my mound!" a voice called.

Bartleby opened his eyes and saw that he had landed on a cushiony pile of leaves and moss. "Going," he mumbled. He didn't wait to find out whose voice it was under the heap.

Seezer was waiting for him on the path. He swung

his head from side to side, as if he wasn't sure what to do next. "Glad to see you sssurvived!" he exclaimed. "A giant tree-leaping lizard, ha! That's a good one."

"Thanks. We'd better get going before anything else happens."

Seezer eyed Bartleby for a moment. Then he flattened himself against the ground. "Climb on my back, and I'll carry you. I believe I sssee the lights of human houses ahead."

Smack! Something crashed into Bartleby's side. He was nearly rolled over onto his carapace.

"Foul ball!" a voice shouted.

Carefully, Bartleby edged his head out. He was surrounded by a thicket of tightly woven branches. Small purply green leaves covered most of the wood.

"C'mon, Danny! Find the ball!"

"You hit it, Tim. You get it!"

"Me? You're supposed to be the catcher."

"I don't care. That hedge is crawling with poison ivy. I'm not getting that ball."

"Ball? What's a ball?" Seezer hissed. With his flat, powerful body, he'd been able to push even farther under the hedge than Bartleby.

"A ball's what just bumped into my shell," Bartleby answered. "And if those boys crawl under here to get it, they're going to find us, too!"

"If they sssee us, they may try to capture us. I couldn't

145

ssstand to be a pet again. Maybe I ssshould try to eat those boys first."

"No, don't!" The idea of eating boys gave Bartleby a funny, fluttery feeling inside. "Leave things to me. Just keep as still as you can." He pulled his head back into his shell and tried to look like part of the hedge.

"Lady! Here, girl. Find the ball! FIND IT!"

"That's right, Lady. Good girl! GET THE BALL!"

Something rustled the branches above Bartleby. It huffed and puffed great breaths of smelly air. It clawed the ground.

"Uff Uff! Me-ball! Me-ball!" The creature stuck her wet black nose under the bush.

Bartleby peered out at an animal with brown-and-white fur and long, floppy ears. He thought for a moment. "Hmmm. Furry . . . jumpy . . . noisy . . . dumb . . . it must be a puppy!" He poked his head out a bit. "I'm not the ball! This round thing's a ball. Take it and go away!"

"Uff Uff! Me-ball! Me-bush! Me-yard!" The dog shook her ears. "Uff Uff! Me-boys!"

"I don't want your ball, or your bush, or your yard. And I certainly don't want your boys. I'm just passing through," Bartleby whispered.

"Lady! Bring me the ball! COME ON, GIRL!"

"Uff Uff! Go-way, Green Rock!" The puppy opened its jaws and grabbed a branch just above Bartleby's shell. She shook the wood until leaves began to fall.

"I'm not a rock, I'm a turtle. And I can't go now," Bartleby explained. "I have to wait until it's dark. I'm on my way to—" He fell silent as he felt the vibrations of boys approaching.

"What's the matter, Lady? Can't you reach the ball?"

"Come on, Danny. Maybe we should forget it. What if Lady gets poison ivy?"

"Don't be a dummy, Tim! Dogs don't get poison ivy."

"Not even on their noses?"

Bartleby gathered his courage and stuck his head all the way out. He nudged the ball toward the bobbing black nose and the snarling mouth. "Here, take it. Please."

The puppy opened her mouth wide. Bartleby could see her bright pink gums. He pulled in his head and waited.

"LADY, COME ON ALREADY!"

The puppy snatched the ball. "Uff Uff!" she warned as she began backing out from under the hedge. "Uff Uff Uff!"

Bartleby let out a grunt of relief. "Yes, I know," he assured her. "*Your* ball. *Your* yard. *Your* boys."

Across the School Yard

29

Under a sky of hazy moonlight, Bartleby and Seezer crawled onto a well-worn field. At the center was a long, brick building with many windows. Could this be the school yard Junket had mentioned? The place where the crow ate the children's lunch crusts? The twins, Jeff and Josh, had gone to school each morning. They'd worn bags on their backs that had made them look a bit like turtles. But here, at night, there wasn't a single child.

Bartleby looked at the strange shapes standing at one end of the field. He recognized the swings because there'd been one in Davy's backyard. But instead of just one swing, this place had a whole row. There were also shiny things that slanted like hills. Bartleby knew about them, too. Davy had pushed him down one just like it. Bartleby had skidded and flown off into the dirt.

Seezer groaned, rousing Bartleby. "I'm ssstarving. I've eaten only a few worms and mosssquitoes sssince we left the water place. And my ssskin is so dry, it hurts. I miss water and mud. I don't think I can go any farther."

Bartleby was dry, too. Dry and hot and very tired. "Through the woods. Past the humans' houses. Across the school yard. Beyond the field of holes. Over the great road," he chanted. "I don't think we have too much longer to go. But we must reach the far side of this place before it turns light again. We can take cover in that line of bushes that borders the field."

A thick cloud drifted over the moon, darkening the night. "I can't sssee any bushes," Seezer complained. "Sssuppose we're not going in the right direction?"

In spite of the heat, Bartleby shivered. "Just keep moving. I know the way." He tried to make himself sound confident.

They reached a place where no grass grew. Instead, there was only a dusty, squarish stretch of dirt outlined in very straight white lines.

"This dirt is ssstriped like a ssskunk," Seezer said. "And I wonder what this black thing is doing here."

Bartleby nudged the thing with his head. It felt hard yet springy. "My boys had something like this in the yard. Davy put me on it once. I think it's called a home plate."

"Ahh, home." Seezer stopped crawling. He snorted a great snort and beat his tail on the black thing. "The dust here is making me choke. I can't go any farther." He folded his legs and dropped his long, flat head onto the bare earth.

"But we can't just stay here. There's nowhere to hide. We'll be caught!" Bartleby nudged Seezer's head, but the alligator wouldn't move.

In fact, it seemed as if Seezer could no longer hear him. He lay as flat and still as the thing called home plate. Bartleby gave up and settled down to watch over him. With his shell pressed tightly against his friend's side, he fell into a dreamless nap.

A rumbling like the growling of a big dog vibrated Bartleby's shell. It was followed by a noise like the cracking of a giant branch. Bartleby stretched out his neck. "Seezer, wake up! Listen!"

Seezer emitted a tiny snort. "Can't."

Bartleby nudged his friend's leathery side. "Try! Please."

With a great effort Seezer raised his head. He opened his eyes. "I feel the air tingling!" he whispered excitedly.

Another crack sounded. Slowly, soft drops began to fall. They made a *plipping* sound on Bartleby's shell. He held his head out. He opened his mouth. The water tasted light and pure.

Seezer swished his tail back and forth. The rain began to fall faster. Harder. It pelted the swings. Before long it turned the dirt to mud.

"Ssslippery, ssslimy, sssensssational mud," Seezer crooned happily. "I feel like digging a hole!"

"Here?" Bartleby asked. "Now?"

"I sssurely must," Seezer answered, his snout already

pushing at the softened dirt. "My mama was famous for her 'gator holes." Slowly, he began turning in a circle. Scraping with his powerful tail. Digging with his sharp claws. Scooping with his long, flat snout.

Bartleby settled himself atop home plate to watch.

It wasn't very long before a dent in the earth began to form around Seezer. He began turning faster. Mud flew. His dent became a basin. Rain began to collect inside it.

"It looks wonderful," Bartleby said. "Deep enough for an excellent mud bath."

Seezer grunted. A large lump of mud sailed out of the hole. And another and another. The basin became a hollow. The rain kept collecting.

"The water's nearly deep enough to swim in!" Bartleby exclaimed.

Seezer grunted and turned and grunted and turned. The rain ran in rivulets down into the hollow. At last, when the moon began to sink in the sky, the hollow was a hole—a 'gator hole filled with water and mud.

Seezer splashed his tail. "You can come ssswim now," he said proudly. "You can ssswim and remember our water place."

Bartleby crawled to the edge of the hole and looked in. "This is the loveliest sight I've seen in days," he said. "Thank you, Seezer." He slipped into the water and paddled back and forth, back and forth, until the first ray of sunlight appeared. Then the two friends hurried out of the hole and across the field to hide under the bushes.

The Field of Holes

30

In the center of a small, green oval of water, Bartleby was soaking up sunlight. How surprised he'd been to find this water place. There had been no tangled thicket or stand of tall blades to hide it. The water was as open as an unblinking eye.

The ground here was strange, too. All around were low, rounded hills, covered in the shortest, tightest grass Bartleby had ever seen. Plus, there were some holes. They were muskrat-size holes, although not nearly as deep. Still, you had to be careful about them, especially in the dark.

It was also strange, Bartleby thought, that he and Seezer appeared to be the only creatures who had found the little pond. Except, that was, for the plump orange fish that swam back and forth, round and round. They were the most boring fish Bartleby had ever seen.

Their dullness didn't keep Seezer from gobbling

them up. "A ssstupid meal is an easy meal," he said. "Besssides, I'm awfully sssick of eating insssects." With a snap of his jaws, he disappeared under the surface.

Perhaps it would be good to spend a day resting and gathering strength, Bartleby thought. With the sun's rays directly overhead, he began to feel pleasantly muzzy. He let his eyes close halfway.

Suddenly, he heard a sharp *clack*. The air above him began to vibrate. He raised his head and saw a perfectly round egg flying through the air. Quickly, he pulled his head in. With a hard splash, the egg smacked the water and sank to the bottom.

What kind of bird lays its eggs while flying? Bartleby wondered. He knew Mother Wak would never drop her egglets so carelessly. He looked up. The bright sky was empty. Not even a sparrow flew overhead.

Seezer popped up from the water holding the egg delicately between his jaws. "This is the ssstrangest egg I've ever sssseen," he said, rolling it onto the island. "The bottom of the water is covered with them."

Bartleby plodded over and leaned his head against the eggshell. "I don't hear its heart beating." He peered at it more closely. Instead of being smooth, the shell's surface was dimpled everywhere.

Another *clack*, and another egg crashed into the tiny island. "It didn't even break!" he exclaimed. "The bird that lays these must be tough and fierce."

"Maybe it's not a bird," Seezer whispered. "It could be another kind of creature, although I know that alligator eggs don't look like this."

"I don't think turtle eggs do, either," Bartleby said, though he'd never actually seen one. He thought about other kinds of egg-laying creatures. Fish, frogs, lizards—and snakes. "I hope they're n-n-not snake eggs," he stammered.

They fell silent as a different kind of vibration reached them. Two large humans were approaching the pond. Each one was carrying a stick with a flipper at the end. "I can't find that ball anywhere," the taller one said. "It must have landed in the water."

"So that egg is not an egg—it's a ball!" Bartleby murmured. "What a small ball for such large creatures."

"Are you sure it isn't on that island?" the other human asked.

"I can't see it."

"Take off your shoes, why don't you? Wade in and check."

"Are you kidding? I heard they've got alligators in this pond."

Both humans let out large bursts of noise that sounded like crows cawing.

"I suppose I'll have to play another one." The taller human reached into a pocket and set down another egg-ball. He drew back his stick and *crack*—the ball went sailing over the grass. The humans began walking after it.

"They know you're here!" Bartleby whispered to Seezer after they'd disappeared. "We'll have to leave tonight before they come back."

"I don't care! There are ssso many of those egg-balls at the bottom, I can hardly find any mud to dig in. And the fish here are plump, but they don't have much flavor."

"Soon you will have all the fish you can eat. Tonight we'll search for the great road. Junket said the traveling water is on the other side." Bartleby left out the part about the fast cars and the squashed carcasses of the creatures who came too close.

The Great Road

31

When he heard the owl begin to hoot and felt the vibrations of bats swooping low, Bartleby crept out of the brush. Before him the road waited. It was even darker than the night sky—and for a while it was just as quiet. But then cars would come. Their lights threw glowing yellow stripes that made Bartleby squint.

Beside him, Seezer closed his eyes halfway as if he were in ecstasy. "I sssmell the ssscent of traveling water! You were right. We are almost there."

Bartleby opened his mouth and inhaled. The smell that wafted across the road was different from the scent of the big water place. It was sharper and fresher. The scents of new plants and new creatures were mingled with others he knew and loved. It was the most wonderful-smelling water he had ever known.

"I must bathe in it!" Seezer exclaimed.

"I must feel it flow over my shell!" Bartleby agreed.

He turned his head from side to side to look for cars—and saw a dead squirrel nearby.

"I sssuppose that the poor creature was on his way to the traveling water, too," Seezer whispered. "Sssurely a sssquirrel is ssspeedier than either of us. I don't sssee how we'll ever make it." Hunkered down in the dirt, he looked tired and frightened. Not at all like the fierce creature he'd been in the big water place.

"Seezer must get to the river soon, so he can regain his strength," Bartleby said to himself. He rested quietly by the roadside, watching the cars pass. And thinking.

"If we cross one at a time, we are less likely to be noticed," he said finally. "And we can act as lookouts for each other. I'll watch one direction and you watch the other. When both ways are clear, you will go first."

Seezer flicked his tail back and forth. "Me? But why?"

"Because you are faster and braver. When I see you on the other side, it will give me confidence." Bartleby nudged the alligator's hide. "Good luck, friend!"

"I will sssee you on the other ssside."

Bartleby gazed alertly in one direction. With his webs, he felt the road for vibrations. Seezer gazed in the other direction. He held his tail straight out behind him. Three cars zoomed by one way. Two cars whizzed by the other way. Their lights blazed like angry eyes.

Finally, all was dark and silent.

"Now!" Bartleby exclaimed.

With his tail, Seezer catapulted himself onto the road. On his short, powerful legs, he hurtled across the wide, sticky blacktop. He was well on the other side when the next car streaked by.

His victorious bellow made Bartleby's webs quiver with relief. "Can you see it?" he called to Seezer.

"Yes! It is just down this embankment. It's not very wide, but it's flowing sssplendidly."

Eagerly, Bartleby placed his forefeet onto the road.

"Be careful!" Seezer warned. "I feel sssomething coming."

Bartleby stepped back and pulled his head in. Wheels rumbling, two cars raced by. Then it was silent again.

"It ssseems clear now," Seezer called.

"Here I come!" Bartleby crawled onto the road and began scrabbling over the blacktop. It felt hard and un-friendly under his webs. It scraped at his plastron. It was smeared with the bodies of insects.

He concentrated on keeping up a steady pace. It seemed like forever until he reached the two yellow lines in the middle of the road. He crawled eagerly over them and began his trek across the other half.

Under his webs, Bartleby felt the road quiver. Quickly, the quiver became a quaking. He stopped crawling.

"Hurry! Sssomething's coming!" Seezer bellowed.

Bartleby turned his head and saw two light beams sweeping the highway. He pulled his head into his shell.

"Don't ssstop!" Seezer roared. "Come quickly!"

Bartleby poked his head out. He tried to hurry, but the light beams were coming closer. Behind them he could see spinning black wheels.

"Bartleby! I'm coming!!!" Seezer roared as he sprang back onto the road.

"No, stop!" Bartleby stared in horror as his friend raced toward him. In another moment, he felt Seezer's powerful tail bat his shell.

Bartleby was flying, flying, flying—across the black-top at a terrific speed. He heard a sickening thud. A terrible groan. Then he crashed into the brush.

Tail's End

32

Sunlight seeped into Bartleby's shell and made his head hurt. He kept his eyes closed and tried to move his neck. A sharp jolt shot along his carapace. Was his shell cracked? He poked his feet out and pressed them lightly against the ground. The soft earth he felt told him he was no longer on the road.

A memory. Once again he saw Seezer's tail swinging, batting him out of the path of the lights and wheels. He heard the thud. *Seezer!* What had happened to him?

In the darkness of his shell, Bartleby was certain he knew the answer. It made him want to stay closed up forever.

"Oh, Seezer," he whispered. "I tried to be a good traveling companion, but I wasn't brave enough or fast enough. I'm sorry I let you down."

For a long while he lay perfectly still in his shell. Even if he could move, he thought, where would he go? He didn't care about the traveling water anymore.

He had no idea how much time had passed when a breeze woke him. Bartleby heard flapping sounds. And cawing. Something tapped on his shell.

Slowly, he edged his head out. A crow jumped back in surprise.

"Go away, I'm not dead yet," Bartleby told it.

"Sorry." The crow pecked at the ground. "Er, what about that, er, creature down the road? Know if it's dead? Didn't want to get too close—just in case."

"Stay away from him!" Bartleby tried to sound fierce, but his voice came out weak and thin. "That creature is my friend. He is tired because we've traveled such a long way."

"Looks dead to me. Sometimes hard to tell, though. Er, definitely got something wrong with his tail." The crow pecked at a mite under its wing.

"Even without a tail, he could eat you in a snap," Bartleby warned. "You'd better fly away before he wakes up and I tell him you've been asking about him."

"Er, no need for that! I'm going." The crow fluttered its wings. "I'll be back to, er, check up on you." It cawed at its own joke as it flapped away.

Bartleby stretched his aching neck out and squinted down the blacktop. He saw Seezer lying motionless on the gravel at the side of the road. Slowly, he ran his eyes along the length of Seezer's body. And felt his heart stop beating.

With a great effort, Bartleby struggled up on his webs.

Step by step, he plodded down the gravel by the side of the hot blacktop.

"Seezer." Bartleby nudged his friend's head, but there was no response.

"Seezer, please wake up. Please try!" Bartleby leaned up against the limp, still body. Sorrow gripped him. He wished he could make his eyes rain the way Davy's had.

Slowly, he turned away and crawled down to the alligator's tail. The end of it was missing. The sight of the sticky blood made Bartleby's head feel light and floaty. He wanted to slip into a turtle nap that would take him away.

But something was calling to him. It was a low-pitched, chattering sound that made Bartleby think of birds. Except it wasn't coming from the sky. It was coming from the bottom of the embankment.

Bartleby opened his eyes and looked down the grassy slope. It was a softly rolling drop. Sure enough, the traveling water was at the bottom. Glistening, streaming water that flowed over pebbles, rocks, and sticks. Water that bubbled and murmured cheerfully, as if nothing were wrong.

In spite of his grief, Bartleby felt a tiny pull inside. And the stirring of an idea. "Seezer, you will reach the traveling water," he said firmly to his friend's lifeless form. "You will begin the journey home today." Then he leaned his carapace up against the alligator and began to push.

Bit by bit, Bartleby moved Seezer's body toward the edge of the embankment. First his head. Next his middle. Last, his shortened tail. Then Bartleby returned to his friend's head and started the pushing again. He kept at his task until, with a final shove, Seezer's body began rolling down the side of the embankment. With a light splash, it dropped into the water. Bartleby felt as if his own heart had dropped in after it.

Exhausted, he plodded down the slope. At the edge of the traveling water he stopped and inhaled its rich fragrance. He watched petals and leaves being swept along in the lively current. He imagined Seezer gliding with the flow, tail waving happily. Going home.

With a forefoot, Bartleby tested the temperature. How cool and refreshing the water felt! It was inviting him . . . drawing him forward. Bartleby gave himself up to the feeling and entered the stream.

He was surprised at how shallow and narrow the traveling water was. He could easily touch the many rocks at the bottom. In just a few strokes, he could reach either of the grassy banks. And the water was quite bouncy! As it lifted him up, Bartleby felt as light as a lily petal.

Seezer's dark form was already beginning to drift away. Bartleby began swimming after it, alert to the newness of moving with the current. Carefully he paddled up as close as he could to the alligator's ear. "Good-bye, friend," he whispered. "I'll never forget you." For the last time, Bartleby bumped up against Seezer's body. Then he paddled away.

How good the water felt against Bartleby's webs! How energized he felt as it flowed over his carapace! How glad he was to be alive! He began swimming faster.

"Ssslow down," a voice rasped. "Wait for me."

At first, Bartleby wasn't sure he'd heard correctly. He thought it was the water bubbling. Or a creature he'd failed to notice. With a great effort, he pushed against the current and turned around to look.

Seezer was gliding toward him, eyes open, jaws slightly parted. "Traveling water is the energy of life," he said. "This time, you sssaved me. Thank you, Bartleby of the Mighty Mississippi."

Bartleby was so full of joy, and pride, and hope, he couldn't speak. For now, he would have to let the murmuring water be the sound they shared. He slowed his pace to let Seezer catch up with him. And together, the two friends began their journey.